I0690022

Witch Hunt

Witch Hunt
A Nathan Perry Mystery

CAROL PREFLATISH

Copyright © 2022 by Carol Preflatish

All rights reserved. No portion of this book may be copied or transmitted in any form, electronic or otherwise, without express written consent of the publisher or author.

Cover design: Stephen Zimmer

Cover art in this book copyright © 2022 Stephen Zimmer & Seventh Star Press, LLC.

Editor: Stephen Zimmer

Published by Seventh Star Press, LLC.

ISBN Number: 978-1-7368125-6-3

Seventh Star Press

www.seventhstarpress.com

info@seventhstarpress.com

Publisher's Note:

Witch Hunt is a work of fiction. All names, characters, and places are the product of the author's imagination, used in fictitious manner. Any resemblances to actual persons, places, locales, events, etc. are purely coincidental.

Printed in the United States of America

First Edition

Acknowledgements

There area few people I want to thank for their help with this book:
Amanda Bary
Nancy Kutz
And
Josh and Katheryn Bowsher

Finally, a huge thank you to Stephen and Holly for their encouragement and faith in me and my writing.

Book Blessing

You are my book
You are my way
Inside is my soul
Each page a step to my goal
I aim to be one
I aim to be pure
To let all hatred out
And allow the light to be endured
So Goddess, my light
Protect every single page
Unto after another book
Unto after this day and age

So Mote It Be.

Author Unknown

Chapter One

Detective Nathan Perry hated his one-week-a-month required uniform duty, thankful today was the last day of it. "Let's take a swing down Main Street," he said to his partner for the week, and best friend, Hank McCoy.

"Good idea. I'm anxious to see how the overflow of tourists from Salem is today." Hank turned left at the next street to head for downtown Mystic.

The men soon had their answer. People were walking on both sides of the street, going in and out of the shops. It looked like the busiest shops were the ones that featured witchcraft novelties.

"Around here, the only thing worse than summer tourist season is Halloween," Hank said.

"Yeah, but think of it this way, we don't work for the Salem Police Department. They've got to have their hands full of quirky people by now. We only have the overflow."

"Want to go to Ginger's for a late breakfast?" Nathan asked.

"Yes. I'm starved."

After leaving downtown, Hank parked in a private parking lot behind the Witch's Brew Café. They entered through the back door, and looked for their usual booth, which they found occupied by two young ladies dressed in black clothes and wearing black lipstick. Instead, they took a booth on the other side of the room.

"Good morning, gentlemen," café owner, Ginger Raines said, approaching their table.

"How do they eat without getting that black stuff all over their faces?" Hank asked, referring to the young ladies.

Ginger laughed. "The same way as women wearing red lipstick. What can I get you two today?"

"I'd like one of your fantastic chicken salad sandwiches with some chips," Nathan said.

"I'll have the same," Hank added.

"Coffee or Coke?"

"Coke," they answered in unison.

"Be right back," Ginger said, and headed to the kitchen.

"What witch holiday is it this time of the year?" Nathan asked, as he looked at all the people dressed in various versions of witches in the busy restaurant.

"I think it's called Mabon, the autumn equinox. I don't really keep up with all of that. I actually just heard someone talking about it at the gas station yesterday. I talked to one of the guys from the Salem PD yesterday, and he said all of the hotel rooms in their town were full."

"Which means our hotels are filling up fast. It's going to be a long Fall."

Hank nodded in agreement. "Let's just hope for a peaceful season this year."

"Here you go, guys." Ginger sat their food and drinks in front of them. A teenage girl working for Ginger followed with their drinks.

"This looks great," Nathan said.

"I aim to please. Should I go ahead and cut you boys a piece of my famous apple pie with a scoop of ice cream?"

"None for me, thanks," Hank said. "My department physical is coming up soon."

"Me either, but could you save a slice for me to take home tonight?" Nathan asked.

"Absolutely. I'll put your name on it," she said.

"I'll stop by after work to pick it up. Thanks."

"Can I get you anything else for now?"

"I think we're good," Hank said, looking at Nathan, who was already taking a bite of his sandwich and nodded in agreement.

Ginger smiled and headed over to another table where a customer was waving to her.

"Does she still clean your house?" Hank asked Nathan.

"Yep, best housekeeper I ever had. She's in and out, and I hardly know she's there. Best thing about it is that a lot of the time, she brings leftovers from the café."

"Five-thirteen – Central Dispatch," the female voice said over Hank's hand-held radio.

Hank picked up the radio. "Dispatch – Five-thirteen. Go ahead."

"Five-thirteen, can you and six-nineteen meet five-ten at Bridge Road at the cemetery just west of Water Street."

"On our way," Hank said into the radio. He looked at Nathan. "I wonder what that's about?"

"I suppose we'll find out when we get there, but I have a bad feeling about it," Nathan said. The two officers stood. Nathan waved some money in the air to catch Ginger's attention, and then placed it on the table. He took one more bite of his sandwich before leaving. Hank took half of his sandwich with him.

Bridge Road, located on the east side of town, started the rural part of Mystic. When they reached the street, they saw two Mystic Police Department patrol cars parked on the side of the road next to the cemetery, emergency lights flashing brightly.

"This can't be good," Nathan said. He and Hank walked up to the other officers standing by their cars.

"That uniform looks good on you, Detective. You should join us working boys more often," Wally, the older of the two officers, said.

"You know I work much harder than you do any day of

the week," Nathan joked.

"That'll be the day. No matter, I'm glad you're here," Wally replied, more serious now.

"What's up?" Nathan asked.

"Take a look over the hill," the younger officer said.

This was the oldest and largest cemetery in Mystic, having some historic gravestones in it. They walked through the oldest part to reach the top of a small knoll, where they stopped. Nathan looked toward the back part of the cemetery and saw it. About fifty yards away, a female body hanging from the tree.

"What the hell?" Nathan said.

"Exactly what I said. Come and see," Wally said, leading the other two officers to the tree. "I thought it was a mannequin at first. I figured this fell under your job description, Nathan."

"Yeah, I'm afraid it does." They reached the tree. Nathan looked up at the body. She was young, with long black hair, and dressed in a white dress. "Anything been touched?"

"No, but I did photograph the tree and body from all sides before calling the coroner."

"How did you find the body?" Nathan asked.

"It was a cell phone call. The dispatcher said the person didn't identify themselves, just that something had happened out at the cemetery. With it being over the hill, we didn't see it at first. You can't see it from the road. Then, we walked over the hill and found her. You know, they say there's a bunch of witches buried out here," Wally said.

Nathan looked at Wally. "Is that true, or just a rumor?"

"It's just something I've heard since I was a kid," he replied.

"Let's keep that to ourselves, okay?" That's all that the public needed to think about, a witch being murdered at the cemetery.

"Yes, sir."

Nathan heard cars stopping out on the highway. "Wally, could you check on the traffic? Your partner might need help, if word got out. I don't want any civilians seeing this. Can you also call Mallory Duncan to come out here? She'll need to collect evidence."

"Yes, sir." Wally walked back toward the road, leaving Nathan and Hank at the scene.

"What do you think?" Hank asked.

"I think we have a sick person running around here. Have we had any animal mutilation complaints lately?"

"Not that I know of, but there could have been some calls that I wouldn't know about. Why?"

Nathan knelt down. Her dress was dirty, like she had been dragged on the ground. A few stains looked like blood, but with her still hanging from the tree, he couldn't see any wounds, other than a few scrapes. "Whoever did this probably tortured the animals first for practice."

"That's a thought."

Nathan saw a man pop over the knoll from the road. He recognized him as the coroner, Vince Scanlon.

Scanlon reached them, and sat his case down. "Gentlemen." He pulled two rubber gloves out of his pocket, and put them on.

"You got here fast," Nathan said.

"I was driving in the area when I got the call."

"Anything you can tell us right away would be a big help, Vince," Nathan said.

"First thing, has this been photographed?"

"Wally said he took some photos."

Scanlon took out his camera. "I better take my own." After he took several photos, he wrote some things down on his clipboard. "We need to get her down, and then call the State Police Crime Unit, and medical examiner. An autopsy will need to be done."

Hank took out his knife, and cut the rope that was tied near the bottom of the tree. Nathan and Scanlon held onto the rope, lowering the body down on a clean tarp that had spread on the ground.

Scanlon looked closer at the body. "There's no way to tell if the hanging is the cause of death until an autopsy is done."

"You think someone thought she was a witch?" Hank asked.

Scanlon looked up at the tree. "There hasn't been a witch hanged since 1692."

"Great, all we need is for the public to think a witch was hanged. We'll have every cult groupie around flocking to Mystic," Nathan said.

"As if we don't have enough already?" Hank added.

"I guess so. Wally said he always heard there were witches buried in this cemetery. Do you know anything about that?" he asked Scanlon

"That's always been the rumor. You could check at the library about it." Scanlon took her liver temperature.

"How long do you think she's been here, Vince?" Nathan asked.

"It looks like less than twenty-four hours. The state's medical examiner will be able to give you a better answer."

Nathan could hear more cars and voices from over the hill. "Damn. Hank, will you go remind Wally and James not to say anything about this to the public, especially about witches, if they haven't already?" Nathan asked.

Hank took off toward the road, while Nathan stayed with Scanlon.

"I guess I better call the Crime Scene Unit." Nathan took his phone out and made the call. After finishing the call, he put his phone back in his pocket. "CSU will be here in about an hour." He then saw a small woman appear over the hill, walking toward them carrying a couple cases.

"Good afternoon, gentlemen. What do we have here?"

"You don't waste any time do you, Mallory?" Nathan said to Mystic's only crime scene technician.

"Let me guess, the state's CSU won't be here for about an hour, right?" She took the camera out of her backpack.

"Right."

Like Scanlon, Mallory started taking photos of the body from all sides. "Did anyone get photos of her hanging from the tree," she asked.

"I did," Scanlon replied.

"Can you email copies?"

"I can. Nathan, if you need to go, I'll wait for CSU to get here. I'll also take care of calling the state medical examiner," Scanlon said.

"I would like to check on some missing person reports," he said. "Mallory, make sure you scour a large area around the tree to see if you can find anything relevant. Oh, and can you check to see when the cemetery was last mowed?"

"Yes, sir."

"I'll make sure Hank stays with you until the body is removed." When Nathan got back to the road, he found several people were already gathering on the side of the street. He stopped to talk to Hank. "I'll send some other officers out here to help secure the site, and to keep sightseers away. Stay with Mallory and Scanlon until the body is removed."

"Thanks. I'll make sure no one bothers them."

" I need the car to get back to the office. Would you mind catching a ride back to town with another officer?"

"Sure, no problem," Hank said.

Back in town, Nathan headed straight to the records clerk at the police department. "Sarah, you busy?" he asked from the doorway to her office.

"For you, I always have time," she replied.

Blonde and blue-eyed, Sarah Daniels always had her eye on Nathan, but he had a rule about not dating anyone he worked with at the department. He entered her office, and sat down. "Has anyone filed any complaints recently about missing pets, or animal mutilations?"

"Eeww, gross." She made a horrible face, then got serious. "How recent?"

"Say in the last month."

She started typing on her computer. "You know, you can look this up on your computer, too."

"I know, but you're so much better at it than me," he said, smiling.

Sarah smiled back, blushing. "Looks like we've had two complaints about missing dogs. One was two weeks ago. The other three weeks ago."

"Were the animals found?"

She looked at her screen. "Not that's been reported."

"What about mutilations?"

"No, nothing like that, but we wouldn't necessarily have records on that," she said. "Actually, I'm surprised we had the missing dog reports. Animal Control usually handles those complaints."

"Can you look up their reports?" he asked.

"No. We don't have access. They have their own computer system." She wrote something down on a piece of paper and handed it to him. "Here's their number."

"You know their number without looking it up?"

"You wouldn't believe the things I know," she said rather seductively.

"You have been a big help, Sarah. Thanks."

"Anytime, and I mean ANY time." She winked.

Nathan decided he should leave before this went any further. He would check the missing persons reports himself, and call Animal Control. Before going to his office, he stopped by the break room for a cup of coffee.

He filled a cup, and started to his office, but just as he was about to step out of the room, Police Chief Paul Cabot walked in.

"Perry, I'm glad I caught you. I heard about the incident at the cemetery. What do you know so far?" the chief asked.

"It's a little early to know much. Mallory is still at the scene, and the State Crime Scene Unit is on the way. The coroner will send me his report as soon as he's finished his part of the investigation."

"This won't be good for the tourist season."

"No sir, it never is." No matter what the crime, it was never good for the tourist season, as far as Chief Cabot was concerned.

"As soon as the mayor gets wind of this, she'll be demanding answers, and quickly. I don't have to tell you what will hit the fan when the press finds out."

"No sir, you don't. I've already thought of that," Nathan said.

"And, just what do you plan to do about it?"

"Well, I plan on walking to my office, sit in front of my computer, and pull up some missing person reports. Then, I'm going to go home, change out of this damn uniform, get something to eat, and probably come back here to wait for the coroner's preliminary report, sir."

Nathan knew he would regret that little speech later, but at this point he didn't care. He knew he would be on the chief's shit list again, but it wouldn't be the first time, and it probably won't be the last.

"Keep me informed," the chief said, leaving the break room.

Nathan took a deep breath, slowly letting it out. It had been a long day already, and it looked like it was going to be a long night. In his office, he took a seat at his desk, sat his coffee next to the computer, and brought up the missing persons database.

While reading through the reports, his computer dinged, indicating he had received an e-mail. It was from Vince Scanlon, and contained a very preliminary report on the body. Female, about five foot, six inches, age in her early to mid-twenties. With a click of the mouse, the printer shot out a copy of the report, which contained only a few more details. Now, he had something to go on, even if it was only a small bit of information. He picked up his phone, and made a call.

"Animal Control, how can I help you?"

"This is Detective Perry from the police department, I need to find out if you've had any complaints about missing or mutilated animals, say within the last month?"

"One moment." He was placed on hold.

"This is Amanda Donaldson, Animal Control Officer. I understand you need information on some reports?" she asked.

"Yes, any missing or mutilated animal reports within the last month."

"Why do you need this information?"

"I can't give you details, but it's part of an investigation I'm doing."

"You know, we do our own investigations on cases like this."

Nathan sat back in his chair, loosening his uniform tie. "I realize that. I'm not investigating any of your cases. However, it could be a part of an investigation I'm conducting. If you could just please send me those reports." He gave Officer Donaldson his email address, then ended the call.

A few hours later, he was still waiting on the reports from Animal Control while reading over copies of ten regional missing person reports. He heard someone clearing their throat at the door. He looked up, and saw Sam Denzinger. "What is Massachusetts' top state police detective doing at my door?"

"I heard a call go out for our CSU to come for a body in Mystic. I was in the neighborhood, and thought I'd stop by. What's with your uniform?" Denzinger asked.

"My monthly obligation. I intended to go home and change clothes, but I'm waiting for a call," he said. "In the neighborhood, huh?"

"I was on my home to Salem." Denzinger sat down in front of Nathan's desk. "Honestly, I didn't want to go home yet. My wife's pushing me to retire."

"You going to do it?" Nathan asked.

"Not anytime soon, but I have been keeping it in the

back of my mind."

"What will I do without you?" Nathan joked.

"You'll do just fine. What do you know so far on your body?"

"She was lynched." He handed Sam a copy of the coroner's report.

"That's not good. Have you identified her?"

"Not yet. Mallory took fingerprints. I'm hoping your CSU team can get a match," Nathan said.

"I'll see if I can put a rush on it. As always, they're pretty backed up."

"I also printed off ten missing person reports on females that have disappeared within thirty miles of Mystic that match the vague description we have of the victim. I was just getting ready to go to dinner. Want to join me?"

"It's tempting, but my wife would be jealous if I spent too much time with you," Denzinger joked back, handing the report back to Nathan. "I'd like to help with the investigation, if you don't mind."

"I welcome the help. Can you come back tomorrow morning?"

"I'll be here. Thanks." Denzinger got up, and left the office.

Nathan put the reports into the desk drawer, locked it, and headed out the door himself. He needed to get out of that uniform. However, as he stepped into the hallway, he ran into Mallory. "Are you just now getting back from the scene?"

"I've been out there all day," she said. "I had to scour the cemetery myself."

"Sorry, but I knew you'd find things my officers would miss. Did you find anything?"

"Yes, maybe. I don't know if they are connected to the case, but I found some candy wrappers not far from the tree. I also found a black cloth purse behind another tree nearby. It had a note in it."

"Where's the note?"

"CSU took it to check it for fingerprints, but I took a photo of it first." She showed him the photo on her camera.

"*For those who fail to follow, death will become you.* Sounds like a threat to me," Nathan said. "Was anything else in the bag?"

"I don't know. CSU took everything with them before I could see anything else. They said they would tag all of it, and send it back when they're finished. I also found some cigarette butts and a lighter, but CSU took those too. I looked for footprints, but the ground was too hard for any."

"Did the state CSU find anything themselves?"

"They didn't even look, just took my evidence." she said.

"Will you email me an inventory list of what you found?"

"I will. First thing in the morning. I'm heading home."

"Thanks, Mallory."

On his way home, he stopped by Ginger's café to pick up his dinner and dessert. Inside, he took a seat the counter, and studied the menu in front of him.

"Eating in or taking out tonight?" Ginger asked, when she approached with a pot of coffee.

"I'm taking it home tonight, but I could sure use a cup of coffee while I wait."

"Sure thing, Sugar," she said, reaching under the counter for a cup, and pouring it full.

He took a drink. "You have the best coffee around, Ginger. Much better than that expensive stuff from the coffee shops."

"You're just saying that cause it's free to law enforcement."

"No, no. I'm telling the truth."

"Well, you're the best too. Now, what can I fix you for supper?"

"Do you have any broasted chicken left?"

"I sure do. We just took a batch out of the roaster a little while ago. Do you want the mashed potatoes to go with it?

"That would be perfect."

"Anything else? Slaw, green beans, chowder?"

"No, I think chicken and potatoes will be plenty for me tonight. Oh, don't forget my apple pie."

Ginger clipped the order onto the rotating wheel in the window between the counter and the kitchen. "Order up," she called to the cook, then turned back to Nathan. "So, what's the crime of the day?"

"You know I can't talk about that," he said.

"Yeah, I know, but I can still ask. Someday, you might just tell me."

"You can ask, and yes, someday I might tell you, but not tonight. Ginger, do you know much about witchcraft?"

She laughed. "I bet I hear that question twenty times a day from the tourists, but I never thought I'd hear it from you. I know enough about it to be able to direct the tourists to the right place in town. What do you want to know?"

"I'm really not sure. Is anything going on in the witch community right now?"

"Boy, you really don't know anything. How long have you lived here?"

"You know I've lived here most of my life, but I was never interested in that sort of thing," he said.

"But you are now? Hmmm, that means you're either investigating something involving witches, or you're dating one. Which is it?"

Ding.

"Your order's ready, Ginger," the cook called from the window.

"Saved by the bell, literally," Nathan said.

He took another drink of coffee, and dug out his wallet to pay for his meal.

"Here you go, Sugar. I put that piece of apple pie in a separate bag, and a little carton of ice cream," she said, placing the bags on the counter. "So, which is it, a case or a girl?"

"Thanks, Ginger. This will really hit the spot tonight." He handed her a twenty, not bothering to answer her question. "Keep the change."

"Thanks, Nathan. I'll be by your house Friday afternoon to clean. Will that be a good time?"

"That'll be fine. I'll be at work, but you have a key. One more question, who in town should I talk to about witchcraft?"

Ginger thought for a few seconds. "You should probably talk to Isabella Osborne. She owns the Magick Potions and Gifts store on Canal Street."

"Thanks," he said.

"Have a good evening," she said, as he walked out the door.

Chapter Two

Before going into the office the next morning, he stopped by the Magick Potions and Gifts store. He opened the door to the establishment, and entered. The bell on the door rang, drawing attention to him.

A typical tourist trap, the mercantile housed everything related to witchcraft, or at least it looked like it did. Shelves were stocked with wands, handmade brooms, capes, candles, herbs, jewelry, statues, spell kits, books, and even a neon sign that read, "*Psychic Readings by Isabella.*"

"Good morning. Can I help you?" A smiling woman stepped through the curtains leading to the rear of the store. Nathan was intrigued with her dressing the part of a modern witch, black dress, long black hair, pale skin, and dark makeup. She reminded him of Elvira, Mistress of the Dark, from television, but with less cleavage.

"Yes, I'm looking for Isabella."

"I'm Isabella, but if you're here for a reading, you'll have to wait. My sales clerk hasn't gotten to work yet. I can't leave the storefront unattended."

"I'm not here for a reading. My name is Nathan Perry, Mystic Police Department." He showed her his badge.

"Oh, I'm sorry, Officer Perry. What can I do for you?"

"It's Detective Perry, and I need some information about witchcraft."

"Well, you've come to the right place. Has someone placed a spell that you need to get rid of?" she asked.

"No, no, nothing like that," he chuckled. "Are there still groups of witches around here that meet?"

"You mean covens. Yes, there are a few. Why do you want to know?"

He ignored the question. "Can you tell me if there are any holidays or ceremonies that witches are observing right now?"

"There are many in each season of the year that witches or Wiccans celebrate. If you want me to answer any more of your questions, you're going to have to tell me why you need to know. This sounds like more than just a casual interest," she said.

"Wiccans?" he questioned.

"Buy a book, if you want to know." She went behind the counter, and handed him a book, Witches and Wiccans for the Neophyte.

"I think I'll do that." He pulled out a twenty-dollar bill, and handed it to her. She gave him some change, and handed the book to him in a plastic bag. "One more question, are you a witch, or Wiccan, or whatever you call them?"

"I told you, no more answers until you tell me what this is about," she said.

"I'm not quite ready for that, but I may be back when I can talk more about it."

Nathan's cell phone rang as soon as he left the store. "Perry," he answered.

"Nathan, are you coming to work today?"

He recognized the voice as Gloria Wheeler, front desk officer at the police department. "Good morning, Gloria. How are you today?" He continued walking to his truck.

"I'd be a lot better, if you were here right now."

"What's going on?" he asked.

"Phone calls have been coming in all morning about what happened at the cemetery yesterday."

"From the press?"

"Yes, but mostly from the residents of Mystic. They saw all the police cars out there, and want to know what it was about."

"What did you tell them?"

"I told them I would check into it. Also, Vince Scanlon called too. He wants you to stop by the funeral home, as soon as you can."

"I'm going to stop there first, and then I'll be in to work. Keep telling anyone that calls about the cemetery that you're checking into it. Thanks, Gloria." Before she could respond, he hung up his phone. He knew he would hear from Gloria about doing that.

Nathan drove over to the funeral home on the west side of town. He found the front door open, and walked inside, finding Scanlon in the office on the right.

"Come in. Thanks for getting here so fast," Scanlon said, beckoning Nathan to the chair in front of the desk.

"Have you come up with anything yet?" Nathan asked, sitting down.

"Nothing definite, but I did want to update you after the crime scene unit left yesterday. Would you like some coffee?" Scanlon asked, getting up to pour himself a cup from the pot on the table.

"Yeah, that would be good. Thanks."

Scanlon poured another cup for Nathan. He held up a small dish with packets of sugar in it, but Nathan waved it off. Scanlon sat back down at his desk, and opened a folder. "The CSU took the things that Mallory found. They're going to look over everything and get back to me."

"Witches were hanged in that cemetery back in the 1600's," Nathan stated, before taking a drink of coffee.

"They were?"

"I did a little research on the computer yesterday."

"Think someone's trying to send a message?" Scanlon asked.

"It wouldn't surprise me. I hope once we get her identified, it'll explain a lot."

"The State Medical Examiner's Office came for the body late yesterday. With any luck, they will start the autopsy today, but I'm not sure how long it will take to get the results," Scanlon said.

"Detective Denzinger with the state police is going to ask them to bump it up the line? I'd really like to know if she died from the hanging, or if something else caused her death."

"I'd like to know the same thing."

"If there's nothing else, I better get to work now. Thanks for the coffee. I'll take it with me, if you don't mind."

"Be my guest," Scanlon replied.

Nathan left the funeral home. He parked in the rear parking lot of the police department, and entered through the back door, hoping to slip into his office unnoticed. It wasn't meant to be.

"Trying to hide from me?" Gloria said, stepping out of the break room.

"Not at all." He unlocked his office door. Placing the book on his desk, he sat down. "Were you waiting for me?"

"No, I brought your messages down here to put in your box." She handed him a pile of pink phone messages. "You're a popular guy."

"When you're a police detective, being popular isn't all it's cracked up to be." He started looking through the messages.

"You look tired," she said.

"I was up late last night going through missing persons reports."

"Would you like some coffee?"

"I already have some." He gestured to the Styrofoam cup on this desk.

Nathan looked through the messages, and saw one from Sam Denzinger, who had called first thing this morning. It said he was on his way to Mystic, and would arrive in about an hour. He looked at the time on the message, and then at his watch. Denzinger should be arriving at any time. The other messages were typical ones for a police detective, being invited to speak to a local DAR meeting, a store owner calling to see if he figured out who busted his window yet, and his usual call from Dana Tyler wanting a scoop for the paper.

"Good morning," Sam Denzinger said, walking in and sitting down in front of Nathan's desk.

"Morning."

"Anything new on your hanging victim?"

"I studied the missing person reports last night. I couldn't find any that might be her. I visited a local witch shop here in town this morning, and tried to speak with the owner, Isabella Osborne. She wasn't very forthcoming."

"Do you think she knows something?"

"I'm not sure. She seemed willing to talk to me at first, but when I started asking more specific things about any covens around here, she refused to answer anything else unless I told why I wanted to know."

"Did you tell her?"

"No, but I'll talk to her again."

Just then, the intercom buzzed. "Nathan, Dana Tyler is on line two for you. She's asking about the incident at the cemetery yesterday," Gloria said.

"I'll talk to her. Thanks." He looked at Denzinger. "The cat may be out of the bag." Denzinger nodded, and Nathan put the call on the speaker. "Dana, how are you?"

"If you would call me for dinner more often, I'd be a lot better," she said.

A little embarrassed, and not expecting that reply, he didn't even look at Denzinger. He knew what his expression would be. "What can I do for you?"

"I heard there was a body at the cemetery yesterday afternoon. Any truth to that?"

"The cemetery is full of bodies. That's nothing new."

"You know what I mean, Nathan."

"Where did you hear that from?" he asked.

"I can't reveal my source, but it's kind of hard to hide something along a road like that. I understand police cars were everywhere out there, including a crime scene unit from the state police. Actually, it's the talk of the town right now. What can you tell me?"

"How about no comment?"

He could hear her let out a breath in disgust. "Okay, so you won't give me any information. Will you at least confirm that a body was found out there, and not just a mannequin?"

"Yes, there was a body at the cemetery, no we have not identified who it is yet," he answered.

"Will you call me when you can give me more information?" she asked.

"You will get the official statement sent to you, like always. I promise."

"One more question."

"What's that?"

"Will you call me for dinner soon?" she asked.

This time, Nathan did look at Denzinger. Just as he expected, he was doing all he could to hold in a laugh.

"When this is over, and I am back to a normal schedule, I'll call you for dinner."

"Looking forward to it, Nathan. Keep in touch. Bye."

Nathan pushed the button to disconnect the call. "Well, that didn't take long."

"Are you talking about the body, or taking Miss Tyler to dinner?" Denzinger asked.

"She's attractive, and conveniently nearby when I want to have dinner with someone," he tried to explain.

"No explanation needed." Denzinger held up his hands in surrender. "What's your next step in the case?"

"Mallory said there was a note found in a bag near the tree. Did your techs tell you anything about that?"

"I heard there was a note, but not what it said." Denzinger took a drink of the coffee he brought with him.

"It said, 'for those who fail to follow, death will become you.'"

"Sounds like a threat to me," Denzinger said.

"That's what I was thinking too, but I can't get out of my mind that witchcraft is involved somehow."

"I'd like to take another look around the cemetery, want to go with me?"

"That's what I'm here for. Let's go."

The two men drove out to the cemetery on the edge of town. They walked out to the tree where the body was found. Nathan looked around at the ground under the tree and Denzinger walked around the rest of the cemetery. Finding nothing on the ground, he studied the tree next.

"Why this tree?" Nathan asked." It's a normal-looking tree."

"Perhaps it had the perfect branch to hold her weight. Perhaps it was chosen because of its location, hidden from the road," Denzinger replied. "Were any witches buried here from the 1600's?"

"Yes, hung and buried here."

"There's probably what, about two-hundred graves here?" Denzinger hypothetically asked. "Who would have a record of all these graves?"

"I'm sure someone does. Maybe the town clerk."

Denzinger's phone started ringing. "Denzinger." He listened to the person on the other end of the call. "Okay. Can you email that report to Detective Perry at the Mystic Police Department?" He looked at Nathan. "Right, that's the address. Thanks." Denzinger ended the call.

"What's up?" Nathan asked.

"The Crime Scene Unit identified your body. Her name is Ann Parker. She's from Foxborough. They're emailing you the missing person report right now."

"That was fast."

"What can I say? They like doing favors for me," Denzinger said.

They got back into Nathan's car, and drove back to the police department. During the drive, Vince Scanlon called Nathan with the same news as Denzinger had told him. He added that the medical examiner's office said they would be performing the autopsy the following day.

Back at his office, Nathan opened the e-mail with the report, and hit the print button. "She was twenty-three years old, and single. Her parents filed the missing person report eight months ago." He continued reading.

"CSU would have already notified the parents. At least you won't have that job," Denzinger said.

"I'll still need to contact them. They may know something that will help," Nathan said. "I'll go visit them in person. This report says that her father is the owner of Parker Electronics. That's a pretty big company. I wonder if he has any enemies."

"I'll call the Foxborough police to see if I can get any more info on the case," Denzinger said.

Knock-knock. Nathan looked up, and saw Gloria standing at the door.

"I'm sorry to interrupt, but there's someone here that just filed a missing person report on a girl matching the description of the victim from the cemetery. I thought you might want to talk to her," Gloria said.

"We just received identification of the victim, so it couldn't be the same person. Would you give it to Hank?" Nathan said.

"She asked specifically for you; said you had spoke with her this morning."

"Who's filing the complaint?"

"Her name is Isabella Osborne."

"Tell her I'll be with her in a few minutes," he said immediately.

"Will do." Gloria turned and left.

"Isabella Osborne. Didn't you mention her name when I got here?" Denzinger asked.

"Yes. She's the one I talked to this morning at the witch

store, who wouldn't answer my questions."

"Right, now I remember."

"If you don't mind, I'd like to talk to her by myself, but you can watch from the observation room," Nathan said.

"Show me where to go."

Nathan led Denzinger to the observation room, then went to bring Isabella to the interrogation room. "Right in here, Miss Osborne."

"Thank you. Please, call me Isabella," she said, taking a seat at the table facing the mirrored wall.

Nathan sat across from her with a notepad and pen in front of him. "Officer Wheeler said you wanted to file a missing person report."

"Yes, I do. Remember this morning when I said my employee was late?"

"Yes."

"Well, she never showed up at all."

"So, she's only been missing for," Nathan looked at this watch, "about four hours? That's really not long enough for her to be classified as a missing person."

"But she's never late. She's never missed a day of work. I called her cell phone. There was no answer. That's not like her. Then, I asked my husband to stop by her apartment, and she wasn't there. I know something has happened to her."

He could read her sincerity. "What's her name?" He picked up his pen, ready to write.

"Ann Parker."

"What did you say?" Nathan asked.

"Ann Parker. She's my employee, and she's missing. I know it hasn't been twenty-four hours yet, but I know something has happened to her."

"Miss Osborne." He wanted to tell her, but felt a hesitation. "I'm going to send Officer Wheeler in to take your information, and I will be in touch as soon as possible. I promise I will look into this personally." Before she could say anything, he quickly left the room.

Denzinger met him in the hallway. "Our victim worked for her?"

"In a shop that sells witchcraft souvenirs," Nathan added.

The men walked toward the front of the building. "Why didn't you tell her what happened to Miss Parker?"

"I wasn't ready yet." They reached the front desk. "Gloria, will you go to the interrogation room to take Miss Osborne's report about her missing employee. Don't enter it in the database yet, just put it on my desk. I'll take care of it. Oh, and don't mention anything about the incident at the cemetery to her."

"Okay," Gloria said, grabbing a pad of forms, she headed down the hall.

"I need to get out of here," Nathan said. "Let's go get something to eat."

Denzinger followed Nathan out the front door and to the Hot Dog Grill, two blocks down the street. Off the tourists' path, the business mostly had locals and cops as customers. Nathan and Denzinger took a booth by the front window.

The blackboard behind the counter showed the day's special was the Reuben Dog and fries. "I'll have the Slaw Dog and a Coke," Nathan told the waitress that came to the table.

"I'll take the Special and a Coke," Denzinger added. "So, what's your next step?"

"I want to talk to the victim's parents to get their view on why the daughter of a millionaire was working at a witch shop in Mystic."

"When are you going to Foxborough?" Denzinger asked.

"I'll call them this afternoon, and arrange to meet them later tomorrow. Want to come with me?"

"I wish I could. I have some reports due by the end of the day tomorrow, and need to get them finished. But, make sure you let me know what you find out."

"I will."

The waitress brought their food, and both men dug in as if they hadn't eaten in days.

Witch Hunt

After lunch, Denzinger headed back to Boston. Gloria had put the missing persons report from Isabella Osborne on Nathan's desk. He sat down to read it. Apparently, Miss Osborne didn't know much about Ann Parker, but the report did have her address. He would see if Gloria could go with him to her apartment.

He stepped out of his office and saw Sergeant Donnelly. "Shane, can I speak to you?"

"Sure, what do you need?"

"I got an ID on that female at the cemetery. I also have her address, and was hoping I could take Gloria Wheeler with me to check her apartment out."

"When do you plan on doing that?" Donnelly asked.

"Right now, if I can."

Donnelly looked at his watch. "I suppose I could spare her for a while. Tell her to find someone to fill in for her up front."

"Thanks."

Nathan walked to the front desk. "Gloria, I'm going to go check out Ann Parker's apartment. Sergeant Donnelly said you could go with me, if you want."

"You bet I want." She immediately stood up.

"We can go as soon as you find someone to fill in for you."

"I'll meet you at your office in five minutes," she said.

True to her word, she was at Nathan's door five minutes later. "I'm ready."

Evidence technician Mallory Duncan followed them in her CSU van. Twenty minutes later, they parked in front of the Samhain Apartments. They entered the office where they found a man doing some filing.

"Can I help you?" he asked.

"I'm Detective Perry, and this is Officer Wheeler from the Mystic Police Department. Does Ann Parker live here?"

"Yes, she does. What did she do?"

"Miss Parker was found dead yesterday."

The landlord sat down in shock. "Oh my god. What happened?"

"We're still trying to figure that out. Could you let us see her apartment?" Nathan asked.

"Well, I don't know. Don't you need a warrant for that?"

Gloria stepped forward. "Mr....?"

"Jones, Nick Jones," he replied.

"Mr. Jones, warrants take time to obtain. There's paperwork to do, talking to the judge, and then finding an officer to serve the warrant. Who knows who that officer would be, and how carefully they would go through the apartment? Detective Perry and I are here right now. I can promise you that I will take the utmost care looking through Miss Parker's things. If something did happen to her, time is really of the essence."

"I suppose you're right. Let me get the key," he said.

Gloria smiled at Nathan, who just shook his head, also with a smile.

They followed Mr. Jones to Ann Parker's apartment where he unlocked the door and let it swing open. He started to enter, but Nathan stopped him. Mr. Jones, if you don't mind, could you stay outside?"

"Of course, I'll just go back to my office. Let me know if you need anything else. Will you lock the door when you leave?"

"I will. Thank you." Nathan watched the landlord head back to the office, and then closed the door. He looked at Gloria and Mallory. "We each need to take a room. I'll look around the living room and dining room, Gloria, you look around the kitchen, and Mallory, take the bedroom and bathroom."

They all donned gloves, and started their search. Nathan started in the dining room where there was a hutch with storage and drawers. Anytime he found something that might be helpful, he placed it into a plastic evidence bag and labeled it. Gloria and Mallory did the same in their respective rooms.

After a long period of detailed searching, they all gathered at the dining room table to go over what they found.

"In the bedroom, I found several books about witchcraft," Mallory said. I also found her laptop, and two empty wine glasses. I'll go through the laptop when I get back to the department. There was a black robe with a belt in her closet. It doesn't look like a bathrobe, but more of a ceremonial robe. There was also a locked jewelry box. I bagged it, and will see if I can get it open back at the department too. In the bathroom hamper, I found soiled panties. One looked like it might have semen on it. I'll send it to the state lab to confirm. There were a few other non-essential things that I bagged also."

"I went through the cabinets in the kitchen, and found several bottles of herbs," Gloria said.

"That's not really unusual. Most people have herbs in their kitchen," Nathan voiced.

"These weren't normal culinary herbs. I found Frankincense, Juniper, and Wormwood. These are used in Wicca rituals. There were regular culinary herbs too, that are also used in the rituals."

"How do you know about those herbs?" Nathan asked.

She kind of snickered. "I've lived here all my life. You don't live here, and work for the police department that long, without learning a little about witchcraft. Once you've been back here for enough Halloweens, you'll learn it too."

"Huh. I never thought about that," Nathan said. "I also found books on Wicca and witchcraft in the living room. I found other items, but the two main things I discovered were an address book, and a couple journals she'd been keeping. I only browsed through one of the journals, but I think it may just tie a few things together. I'm going to read through it more thoroughly tonight at home."

While they gathered their evidence together, someone knocked at the door. Nathan opened it to the landlord.

"Detective Perry, Miss Parker's father is on the phone. He told me not to let anyone in his daughter's apartment.

He isn't happy to hear that you're going through her things. Could you talk to him?" Mr. Jones asked.

"Of course." Nathan said.

"We'll load everything in Mallory's van while you talk to the father," Gloria said.

"Thanks. This shouldn't take long." Nathan followed Mr. Jones to the complex's office, and picked up the phone receiver. "Hello. This is Detective Perry. Who am I speaking to?"

"This William Parker. I'm Ann's father, and I understand you're searching my daughter's apartment. How dare you do that without contacting me first."

"Mr. Parker, I'm very sorry for your loss. We had an investigation to conduct to try to find your daughter's killer, and we did not know anything about you, or you would have been contacted," Nathan said.

"I assume you have a warrant to search her apartment, Detective."

Nathan paused briefly before answering. "Yes, sir, I do. Mr. Parker, I really need to speak with you in person. Is there anyway you could come to Mystic tomorrow?"

"My wife is taking this very hard. I shouldn't leave her at this time," he said.

"Would you mind if I came to your home tomorrow instead? It would really help speed up the investigation."

"I suppose that would be fine," Mr. Parker said. After scheduling a time, he gave Nathan his address and the call ended.

Nathan went back to his car. "Gloria, don't let me forget to get a warrant to search Ann Parker's apartment."

"Why? We just searched it."

"Her father asked if I had a warrant, and I told him yes."

Gloria just shook her head, and Nathan drove off.

Chapter Three

The next morning, Nathan and Hank drove south to Boston, and then on to Foxborough.

"Thanks for taking me with you today," Hank said. "It looks to be a long day."

"I can always use a second set of ears, and someone to keep me awake." He took a drink of the coffee he brought with him.

"What does Mr. Parker do for a living?"

"He owns Parker Electronics."

"No kidding. That's a huge company in Massachusetts," Hank said. "It's kind of odd that his daughter turned up in Mystic, don't you think?"

"Exactly what I had thought. Denzinger got her missing person file from the Foxborough Police Department. That's it on the backseat, if you want to look."

Hank reached over the seat for the file, and began looking through it. "Are we going to talk to the detective that ran the investigation while we're there?"

"That will depend on how cooperative the parents are, and how much information we can get from them."

An hour later, they reached the Parker home. "This looks like it," Nathan said. They pulled up to the speaker at the gate and pushed the button. "Nathan Perry, from the Mystic Police Department, here to see Mr. and Mrs. Parker."

The gate slowly opened, and they followed the driveway up to the huge house at the end of the road. "Wow, what a house," Hank said.

When they approached the house, the front door opened, and a man wearing a dark suit stepped out to meet them. "Good afternoon. Mr. Parker is waiting for you in his den. Please follow me."

Nathan and Hank looked at each other as they followed the butler to the den, where they found a tall, gray-haired man sitting on the couch. He stood, and extended his hand. "Hello, I'm William Parker."

Nathan shook his hand. "I'm Detective Nathan Perry from the Mystic Police Department. This is officer Hank McCoy. We're very sorry for your loss."

"Thank you, Detective. Please sit down. Would you like some coffee?"

"Nothing for me," Nathan said. Hank agreed.

The men sat down on the couch and chair that framed the coffee table.

"That will be all, Patrick. Thank you." The butler left the room.

"Detective, can you tell me anything about my daughter's death, other than what the state police told me about how she was found?"

"I'm afraid we don't know much yet. I'm still waiting for the crime lab report," Nathan said. "I was hoping that you might be able to give me some information about Ann."

"What do you need to know?"

"Why was she working in Mystic. It's so far from her home, I would have thought she would have found something closer to here, or even in Boston."

"To be truthful, I haven't seen my daughter in eight months. Until I got the call from the medical examiner's office, I didn't even know where she was," Mr. Parker said.

"What made her leave home?" Hank asked.

"It's such a long story, but the short version of it is that her mother and I were trying to get her to find employment. She has a degree in business management from Boston College, but never used it. All she was doing was sitting home during the day, and partying all night."

"Did she have a boyfriend?"

"She was dating a man named David Anders before Thanksgiving."

"Before Thanksgiving?" Hank asked, as he made a note of the name. "What happened?"

"I'm not sure. She never talked about things like that around me. All I know is that they were seeing each other in November, then all of a sudden, they weren't."

"She disappeared not long after that, correct?" Nathan asked.

"Yes. A month or so later."

"Where can we find David Anders?"

"If I recall, he was a bartender at some bar in town. I don't know which one. Do you think he has anything to do with her murder?" Mr. Parker asked.

"I won't know until I talk to him."

"I'll see what I can find out about him for you."

"I'm sure we can find him ourselves," Nathan said. "Were you supporting Ann financially?"

"Not exactly. She had access to her trust fund. I suppose she was living off of that."

"You haven't checked?"

"No, it's her money," Parker said. "I no longer have access to that information.

"Did she have any interests?" Nathan asked.

"What do you mean by interests, like hobbies?" her father replied.

"Yes, something like that."

"She made jewelry. Oh, and she loved to write. Wrote in her diary every day. Other than going to clubs at night, she didn't have any other interests that I know of."

"Do you know if she had any interest in witchcraft?"

Nathan asked.

"Witchcraft!" a female voice from the door said. "Why on earth would you ask about that?"

Nathan turned around. Entering the room was a silver-haired woman, immaculately dressed, not a hair out of place, and makeup perfectly applied. She clutched onto a cross necklace.

"Dear, please come in and sit down." The lady joined Mr. Parker on the couch. "This is my wife, Margaret. This is Detective Perry from the Mystic Police Department and Officer McCoy."

"How do you do, ma'am? I know this is a bad time, considering your loss, but I'm here to see what you or your husband can tell me about your daughter," Nathan said.

"She was a fine daughter. Perfect in every way."

Nathan noticed Mr. Parker reacted to his wife's statement by looking away.

"I don't know why someone would want to kill her, especially in such a horrific way. You will find who did this, won't you?" Mrs. Parker wiped a tear from her eye with a lace handkerchief.

"We'll do our best, ma'am."

"Detective, I heard you say witchcraft when I came in. Why are you asking about that?" Mrs. Parker asked, again grasping her necklace.

Nathan looked back and forth between the two parents. "We found several things in her apartment related to witchcraft, and I only recently learned that she was employed at a shop in Mystic that sells witch paraphernalia."

"What! William, why would she be working in a place like that?" Mrs. Parker exclaimed, now holding her hand over her heart.

"I don't know, dear. Let's let the detective tell us what he knows."

"Actually, as I said earlier, I don't know much yet. I do know that her employer was in my office this week to report that Ann was missing. I haven't had an opportunity to question her yet, but will do that as soon as I get back," Nathan said.

"Was her employer a--a witch?" Mrs. Parker asked, barely getting the words out.

"I don't know, ma'am." He turned to Mr. Parker. "We'd like to see her room, if we could, and also her journals."

"I don't think that will be possible," Mr. Parker said.

"Not possible? I don't understand."

"Detective, I've hired a private investigator, Mac Dupont, to look into Ann's murder. I'm sure you understand. I'll have the investigator go through her room first, her diaries too, and then contact you."

"You do realize we could get a warrant?" Nathan said.

"The investigator will be in touch. I believe we're finished here. Patrick," Mr. Parker called. The butler appeared in the doorway, obviously listening to their conversation. "Please show the gentlemen out."

Patrick motioned his arm toward the door without saying a word. Nathan and Hank took the hint and left.

"Well, that was interesting," Hank said, as they got into the car. "We need a warrant. There's something they aren't telling us."

"It's going to take time to get a warrant, and by the time we get back here with it, the diaries will be gone, and the room sterilized of any clues. Let's go talk to that Foxborough detective. Maybe he can tell us something."

They drove to the police department in Foxborough and entered the lobby. There was a line at the window, so they had to wait their turn.

"How can I help you?" the officer behind the window asked, when they stepped up.

Nathan showed his badge. "I'm Detective Perry from the Mystic Police Department. I need to speak to Detective Harris, if he's available. It's about a missing person case."

"One moment." The officer picked up the phone and punched a few buttons. He spoke a few words that Nathan couldn't hear, and then turned back to the window. "If you'll have a seat, he'll be with you in a few minutes."

Nathan and Hank sat down near the door to wait. The lobby was larger than the lobby at the Mystic PD, and seemed busier.

"How would you like to work here?" Nathan asked Hank.

"If it had any perks, like Patriots tickets, I'd move here in a minute," Hank said.

"You'd probably have to work traffic control, and never see a game."

Hank chuckled. "You're probably right."

"The door they were next to opened. "Detective Perry?"

"Yes, right here." Nathan and Hank stood. "I'm Detective Perry, and this is Officer McCoy."

"I'm Detective Harris. I understand you are here about a missing person case?"

"Yes, Ann Parker."

The detective's eyes widened. "Come to my office." He led them about halfway down the hall and into his office. "Please sit down. What do you have on her?"

"As you probably know, her body was found in Mystic, and we're investigating her murder. We just left from talking to her parents and were hoping you could fill in the blanks that her parents couldn't, or should I say, wouldn't talk to us about."

"I'll help all I can. What do you need to know?"

"The Parker's seemed cooperative until we told them that she was working in a shop in Mystic that sells witch paraphernalia. After that, they weren't so forthcoming," Nathan said.

"Especially after we asked to see her journals," Hank added.

"Do you know much about the Parker family?" Detective Harris asked.

"I know they own Parker Electronics, but not much more than that," Nathan replied.

"Mrs. Parker is very religious. Mr. Parker, not so much. I suspect she wouldn't want anyone in her circle to know that her daughter worked in a shop like that."

"Mr. Parker said he's hired a private investigator to look into her death, Mac Dupont. Know anything about him?"

"You haven't met Mac, have you?" Harris asked.

"No, why?"

Detective Harris snickered. "Mac Dupont is one of the best PI's in the Boston area."

Nathan felt like he was missing something, but brushed it aside. He was beginning to picture Mac Dupont to be similar to Joe Cassidy, the bumbling PI in Mystic. "Mr. Parker said they hadn't seen Ann for eight months, or know where she was."

"Correct. He filed the missing person report about a month after she left home. Before she left, she pulled the money out of her trust fund via a cashier's check."

"Didn't you check with the bank to see where the money was deposited?" Hank asked.

"I started to. I told Mr. Parker that we could find her pretty quick by doing that, but he said no. I'm not sure how bad he really wanted to find her." Detective Harris got up to close his office door, and returned to his desk. "From talking to some of her friends, I gathered that Ann and her father weren't getting along at all. One of her friends said that he threatened to remove her name from the trust fund."

"That may be what led her take the money and leave," Nathan said.

"That was my conclusion also."

"Did you ever get a look at any of her journals?" Nathan asked.

"No, Mr. Parker wouldn't let me see them."

"What about a warrant?" Hank asked.

"For a missing person case of a twenty-three-year-old that left home on her own? The judge would have never signed it."

"Well, this is a murder investigation now. If he won't

turn them over, we'll have to get a warrant." Nathan stood to leave.

"If there's anything I can do to help, just let me know," Harris said.

"I appreciate that. I'll call, if I need anything. Thanks." Nathan and Hank left the police department and drove back toward Mystic.

Just before getting into Boston, Nathan's phone rang. "Perry ---- We're just south of Boston. We'll can be back in Mystic in about forty-five minutes. Call Detective Denzinger and get him down there too. Has anyone called Vince Scanlon yet? ---- Good, keep me informed, if anything else happens before I get back." He hung up his phone.

"What's up?" Hank asked.

"That was Gloria. There's another body?"

"Another body?"

"A female body was found floating in the harbor. She was dressed in a black robe, like the one we found in Ann Parker's closet."

"Who found her?" Hank asked.

"A boater. You just know that the chief is going to put more pressure on us to solve this."

"Us? I believe that would be pressure on you, my friend," Hank joked.

"No, us. You're officially assigned to this case now."

The smile left Hank's face.

Back in Mystic, Nathan drove straight to the harbor area. The state's Crime Scene Unit van was parked nearby. When he walked up to the group of officers, he saw one of them was Denzinger. "Thanks for coming, Sam."

"Where have you been?" Denzinger asked.

"I was in Foxborough interviewing Ann Parker's parents. Has the CSU found anything yet?"

"There's a diver in the water right now to see what's down there. They've looked around the boardwalk, and didn't find anything there."

"Detective Denzinger, you'll want to see this," a young man called from the edge of the wharf.

The men walked over. A diver lifted a net bag up to the officer on the wharf, who helped pulled the diver out of the water. One of the other CSU officers opened the bag, and brought out a purse. "I don't know that it belongs to the victim, but it was directly below where she was found floating," the diver said.

The officer opened the wet purse, pulling out a plastic zipper bag. Through the bag, the men could see a sheet of paper with printing on it. He handed it to Denzinger, and then looked through the rest of the purse.

"What does it say?" Nathan asked.

Denzinger read the note. "*For those who fail to follow, death will become you.*'"

"That's the same thing the note we found in Ann Parker's bag said." Nathan said.

"The driver's license in the purse says it belongs to Elizabeth Howe," the officer said.

"I know her," Hank said. "She's from here in Mystic, and works at the Mystic Historical Society Museum right over there." He pointed to the multi-floor brick building a few blocks from the harbor.

"Hank, would you go over and see when they last saw her, and anything else they might know about her?"

"I'm on it." Hank walked away.

Nathan turned to Denzinger. "Where's the body?"

"Vince Scanlon took it to his funeral home, and said he'd called the medical examiner from there."

"I guess that's my next stop, then."

"I'll drive, if you want," Denzinger offered.

"That'd be great. Hank," Nathan called to the officer. "Will you take the car back to the department?" The officer gave him a thumb's up signal, and Nathan tossed him the keys.

When the officers reached Denzinger's car, they got in

and drove to the funeral home. Denzinger picked up a file folder from the passenger seat so Nathan could sit down. "Oh, I almost forgot. This is the autopsy report on Ann Parker. They bumped her up as a favor to me. You owe me."

"Thanks." Nathan took the file and read it. "Nothing much out of the ordinary. She was hit on the head, probably knocking her out, and she died from asphyxiation due to the hanging. She had ligature marks around her neck, which we already saw. Official cause of death was ruled as a hanging with complete free suspension of the body. This is interesting. The stains on her clothes was cat blood."

Arriving at the funeral home, they walked inside and found Vince entering his office. Not dressed in his usual suit and tie for his funeral director job, Scanlon wore surgical scrubs. "Gentlemen, come in."

"We're here about our newest victim," Nathan said.

"Come with me then. I'll introduce you," Scanlon joked. He led the two men down a hallway into the embalming room. In the dimly lit room, a body lay on the table.

"How do you work in such a dark room?" Nathan asked.

"I don't." Scanlon turned on the lights, and the room became brighter. He walked over to the body, uncovering just enough of her to reveal the head.

"Have you determined anything yet?" Denzinger asked.

"I looked over the body, and found a bruise forming at the base of her skull." He turned her head to show them. "The state medical examiner found a similar bruise on the back of Ann Parker's neck."

"When will the M.E. pick up Miss Howe's body?" Nathan asked.

"Miss Howe? You've identified her already?" Scanlon asked.

"A purse was found under the pier with her driver's license in it." He showed Scanlon a photo of the driver's license from his phone.

"It sure looks like the same person," Scanlon said.

"It also had the same note in it that was found near Ann Parker's body." Nathan put his phone back in his pocket.

"Interesting. The M.E. is on their way here now, to get the body," Scanlon said. "Can you send me a copy of her license for my file?"

"Sure." Nathan noticed a wet robe hanging nearby. "Is that what she was wearing?"

"Yes," Scanlon said.

Nathan walked over to the robe to look closer. "Ann Parker had a robe just like this in her closet."

"That could be important," Denzinger said.

"It very well could. Vince, keep me informed."

"I always do," Scanlon answered, as Nathan and Denzinger headed out the door.

Denzinger dropped Nathan back at the police department. He was in the middle of writing his report about Elizabeth's Howe's murder when his phone rang. "Perry," he answered.

"Nathan, it's Dana. I'm so glad I caught you in. I received the press release about the body found at the wharf. Have you made an identification yet?"

"If you got the release, you must have seen that it says at the end of it to contact Public Information Officer Gary Patterson with any questions."

"I know, but I thought you might be able to give me--"

"An exclusive, right?" He leaned back in his chair.

"Well, you usually help me out when something like this happens, and with it being the second body found recently, I thought they might be related, and wanted to get a jump on the other media sources."

"What, no questions about the first body?"

"Do you have something new? Of course, I'll take anything you'll tell me."

Nathan laughed. "What's going on? You're never this eager for a scoop."

"I'm sorry. It's just, well, our editor promoted an intern

to a reporter position, and I'm pretty sure she's after my lead reporter job."

"You're not just telling me this to get the information, are you?" he asked.

"No, I wouldn't do that. It's the truth. I swear."

Nathan laughed again.

"Stop that. It's not funny."

"Yes, it is. Okay, the second body we found was female. She had a similar injury to the first body we found. We did find an I.D., but need to notify the family before we release the name. There's no other leads as of this time. "

"You're not telling me everything. I can tell," Dana said.

"Of course, I'm not telling you everything. I can't release all the information on an active investigation. You know that." He started to take a drink of his coffee, but realized it was cold, and set it back down.

"I suppose if that's all I'm going to get; it'll have to do. When you have more, please just tell me, not that little twerp, Emily Haskell."

"I bet someone thought of you as a little twerp when you started working at the paper."

"Never, not me. Bye." She laughed and hung up.

Hank stepped into the office and sat down.

"Did you find out anything at the museum about Miss Howe?" Nathan asked.

"Yes." He set his soda on Nathan's desk, and took out his notebook. "She's twenty-six, been a lifelong Mystic resident, except for the four years she spent at college in Boston. She received a degree in history, and started working at the museum four years ago."

"Does she still have family in the area?"

Hank looked at his notes. "She has an older brother who lives in Boston. Her parents were killed in an auto accident. She lives alone, but no one at the museum knew anything about a boyfriend. The most interesting thing I found out is that she was very interested in witchcraft."

"That is interesting. Funny that her co-workers didn't know if she was in a relationship, but knew of her witchcraft interest."

Hank took a drink of his soda. "One of the ladies there said she rarely talked about her personal life, other than the witchcraft thing. Apparently, she talked about that often."

"Where does she live?" Nathan asked.

"You're going to love this." Hank leaned forward. "She lived at the same apartment complex as Ann Parker."

"It looks like we need to make another visit to those apartments. Did you get the contact information for her brother to make the death notice?"

Hank leaned back into this chair. "Yes. I already made the call to him. He said he hadn't talked to her in about a month."

"Did he notice anything unusual at that visit?"

"He said they had dinner together, and she seemed perfectly fine."

"Did he know about her interest in witchcraft?"

"He was as surprised as the Parkers were about that."

Nathan nodded. "I'll get the warrant for her apartment tomorrow to check her place out and talk to the landlord. Good work. Thanks."

By the end of the day, Nathan was more than ready to go home. As he was going out the back door of the police department, he ran into an officer wearing a green uniform.

"Detective Perry?"

"Yes, can I help you?"

"I'm Levi Sabin. I'm the supervisor at the Animal Control Department. I understand you need to see some of our recent files on animal mutilations."

Nathan shook his hand. He saw Sabin was carrying a large brown folder holding several smaller files. "Yes. It involves an investigation I'm running right now. Are those the files?"

"They are. Can you tell me anything about your investigation? I may be able to help."

Nathan hesitated. He didn't know anything about Officer Sabin, and wasn't sure about divulging anything about the murders. The guy looked almost too young to even shave. "I'm just leaving for the day, but would you like to join me for dinner at the Witch's Brew? We could discuss what I need from your files."

"That's sounds good. I just finished for the day too and could use something to eat," Sabin replied.

Nathan drove over to the café with Sabin following in his city vehicle. They both went inside and sat at a booth in the back, near the kitchen.

"Well, I wondered if you two knew each other," Ginger said, approaching their table. She sat two glasses of ice water down.

"We've known each other all of five minutes," Nathan said.

"Nice. What can bring you two today?" she asked.

"I'll have a dressed cheeseburger with onion rings, and a Coke," Nathan said.

"I'll have the same, but with a large order of fries," Sabin added.

I'll get that right out to you." Ginger left.

Nathan took a sip of his water and looked over at Sabin. "You've read about the body we found at the cemetery?"

"Yes, I have."

"I believe that it may be related to witchcraft."

"That's why you wanted to know about any animal mutilations that we've had."

"Yes. No animals were found with the body, but I just found out that the crime lab found cat blood on her clothes."

Sabin reached for the files he brought. "In the last couple months, we've had four mutilation reports. Before that, none." He handed Nathan the four files.

The files contained detailed reports about the cases, including graphic photos of the animals.

Ginger walked up with their drinks. "Oh my God! What

are you looking at?"

Nathan quickly closed the file. "Sorry. It's for a case I'm working on."

"Just don't let any of the other customers see those photos. It could be bad for business." She gave them their drinks and went back to the kitchen.

He quickly thumbed through the files. "Are all of these cats?"

"Yes, all of them are black cats, and the reports are within a week to ten days of each other. The animals were found near the old dump at the edge of town," Sabin said, taking a drink of his soda.

"It looks like the last one was a week before the murder. These could be a big help. May I keep them?" Nathan asked.

"You can. I made these copies for you."

Nathan closed the file and put them on the seat next to him. "How long have you been with Animal Control?"

"Four years."

"Four years, and you're already a supervisor?"

The cook came up to the table with their food. "Who gets the one with onion rings?"

"That's mine," Nathan said.

He sat their plates down and started to leave.

"Ginger usually brings the food to us. What happened?" Nathan asked.

"I don't know. She told me to bring it out, and said something about being grossed out." He turned and went back to the kitchen. Both officers laughed.

Sabin put some catsup on his fries. "We have a lot of turnover at the department. I've been there the longest, and I don't plan on leaving anytime soon, unless I could get hired as a police officer. That's what I'd really like to do."

"Keep working at Animal Control and watch for openings at the PD. You never know when we'll need new officers." Nathan took a bite of his burger, and swallowed. "You do know that anything I say about the murder case with you cannot be told to anyone else. It's all confidential," Nathan explained.

"I understand." He took a bite of his burger.

Nathan hoped he understood, because he was going to need his help. "Another body was found floating in the harbor. We think it may be related to the cemetery murder."

Sabin swallowed. "Really?"

"I'm going to need you to keep me up to date on any unusual reports you get pertaining to animals being killed. Can you do that?"

Sabin put down his burger, and wiped his mouth with a napkin. "Detective, I may look like a kid, but I'm twenty-four years old. I've been taking night classes at Mystic Community College, studying law enforcement. I've faced angry unrestrained dogs on many occasions, and their owners, which sometimes are far worse than their dogs. Rest assured, I can keep things confidential, and you can count on me, if you need any help." He popped a French fry into his mouth.

"Good. I'm glad to hear it."

They finished their meal, mostly talking about their backgrounds, and upbringing. Both men grew up in Mystic, but at different times. Nathan was impressed, and felt better about Levi Sabin.

Chapter Four

Nathan came into work early the next morning. He needed to assemble his notes after reading thought the journal they found at Ann's home. He also wanted to figure out his next step in the investigation of the second murder. He looked up when he heard someone at his door.

"Mind if I come in?" the chief asked.

"Sure, have a seat." Nathan thought it was unusual for Chief Cabot to ask permission to come in.

He entered and sat down.

"No doubt, you're here about the second murder."

"I am. The mayor has been calling almost every hour for updates. She's not happy about another murder. You know, the town doesn't need this kind of publicity."

"I'm well aware of that, and am doing everything I can to find out who did this. You can tell the mayor that I have a couple interviews set up for this afternoon to get some information on the victims," Nathan said.

"I'll tell her, but I don't know how long she'll be satisfied. Keep me updated." The chief got up, and left the room.

Nathan ran his hand through his short-cut hair, and let out a deep breath. He took the last drink of his morning coffee, and turned to his computer, where he pulled up the day's newspaper with the article about the second murder. Due to lack of information, it didn't include much. Dana would likely be calling again today. He needed to get another statement ready.

As he continued reading, his intercom buzzed. "Yes," he said.

"There's a Mac Dupont, private investigator from Foxborough, here to see you," Gloria said over the speaker.

"I've been expecting him. Could you show him to my office?"

"I sure will." He thought he heard a little laugh in Gloria's voice.

He turned back to his computer to close all of the documents. A few minutes later, he heard someone clear their throat at the door. "Mac Dupont, here to see you," Gloria said.

"Please come in, Mr. Dupont," Nathan said, turning his chair around to face the door. What he saw made him feel about a foot tall when a tall, lanky blonde, wearing jeans, a burnt-orange sweater, and black leather jacket, walked into his office.

"That's Miss Dupont, Detective." She extended her hand to him.

Nathan stood, and shook her hand. "Please sit down." As they sat, he saw Gloria still standing at the door with a smirky smile across her face. "That will be all, Officer Wheeler." Gloria left, but he could hear her laughing all the way down the hall.

"I am so sorry. When Mr. Parker told me Mac Dupont would be coming to see me, I just assumed it was a man."

She smiled. "It's actually Mackenzie, but a lot of people don't want to hire a PI named Mackenzie, so I go by Mac. It's a gender issue, I suppose."

"Do you prefer Mac or Mackenzie?"

"Everyone calls me Mac. I understand there's been another murder similar to Ann's."

Straight to business, Nathan liked that. "Yes, the body was found yesterday floating in the harbor. The medical examiner's office picked up the body late yesterday, so I doubt they have anything yet."

"What similarities exist between the two murders?"

Nathan suddenly noticed her eyes, blue as a clear spring sky. She wore little makeup. She didn't need to. She had a natural beauty about her.

"Detective?"

"What, oh, I'm sorry. Guess I have too much on my mind right now. What did you ask?"

"What similarities exist between the two murders?" she asked again.

"The second body was wearing a black robe, similar to a robe we found in Miss Parker's closet. We also found the same note in the purse of the second victim that we found with Miss Parker."

"You were in Ann's apartment?"

"Yes, we searched it this week."

"Did you have a warrant?"

"We didn't need one. The landlord gave us access, but we did obtain a warrant after the fact. Are you afraid we'd find something we shouldn't?" Nathan asked.

"What did you find in her apartment?"

She evaded his question. He wondered why. Nathan opened a file folder on his desk, and handed her the list of items.

Mac looked over the list. "Did you take possession of all these items?"

"We did."

"What did you find on her laptop?"

"Her files are password protected. We haven't been able to get past that yet. I don't suppose you have her password, do you?"

"No." Mac took out a notebook, jotting down something. "I see you found a journal. What was in it?"

"The only thing in the journal were witchcraft spells. Her notebooks also had information about witchcraft in them." He took a drink of his coffee. "When I mentioned witchcraft to her parents, they became rather defensive. Can you tell me why?" Nathan asked.

"Wouldn't you be upset, if your daughter were involved in witchcraft?"

"I don't know. I don't have a daughter. You?"

"No, I don't have any children, but if I did, I wouldn't want them practicing witchcraft."

"From what I've briefly read, not all witchcraft is bad."

"Could I see the autopsy report?"

Nathan handed her the report. He leaned back in his chair, studying her, while she read over it.

"They're calling the cause of death as a result of the hanging. What about the blow to her head?"

"If you keep reading, you'll see they think the blow to her head knocked her out, and she was then hanged."

"I see." She handed the report back to him. "It's obvious that we're going to be working closely on Miss Parker's case. Her parents are adamant that her killer be found right away. Maybe we could meet for dinner tonight to discuss the case further?"

"That sounds tempting, but I have plans tonight."

"Is your wife expecting you home for dinner?" she asked.

"I'm not married."

"Maybe another night, then." She leaned forward, smiled, and batted her eyes. "Would it be possible for me to get a copy of your files on both murders?"

"Miss Dupont."

"Mac, please," she corrected him.

"Miss Dupont, you may be able to use your sexuality on a lot of your cases, but it won't work here. You'll get a copy of what I want to give you, and nothing more. I'm still the detective in charge of this case."

Displeased, she sat back in her chair. "Mr. Parker told me that I would have the full cooperation of the Mystic Police Department. I would think, as small as your department is, that you would welcome the extra help. If it's inexperience you're worried about, let me assure you, I am very experienced."

Nathan felt the room get warmer, or was it just his own temperature elevating. "I'm sure you are experienced---"

She interrupted him in mid-sentence. "I was a Boston police officer for eight years, two of them with the Homicide Unit. You can check me out, if you like."

He wished she wouldn't say things like that. *An attractive blonde should not be saying it's okay to check her out*, he thought. "I'll get some information on the case put together for you, and will send it to your hotel. I assume you're going to be staying for a while?"

"Yes, but I've not checked into a hotel yet. Can you recommend a good one?"

"The Harbor House is a nice place. Obviously, it's down in the harbor area."

"Sounds good. I'll give it a try. Send my copy of the file down there," she said. Mac rose from the chair, and Nathan did the same.

"I'll walk you out."

"No need. I'm a big girl, I can find my way out." She stepped out of his office, and headed toward the front of the building.

Almost immediately, Hank walked into Nathan's office. "Who was that?"

"That was Mac Dupont, the PI that the Parkers hired."

"No shit? A woman? Well, how about that?" Hank said. "She any good?"

Nathan looked at Hank, and didn't say a word.

"You know what I mean," he clarified.

"She said she worked for Boston PD for eight years, and in homicide for two. I'm going to ask Denzinger to use his contacts in Boston to find out about her," Nathan said. "Are you on patrol today?"

"No, I'm at your beck and call."

"Good, can you call Isabella Osborne? Ask her to come in around ten o'clock, and we can question her?"

"I'll do that. I don't suppose you've heard anything from the state about our latest victim, have you?" Hank asked.

"Not yet, if I don't hear something by this afternoon, I'll give them a call." Nathan picked up his coffee cup, and remembered he had finished the last of it earlier. "I need more coffee."

The two men headed down toward the break room, when Nathan saw Mac Dupont approaching them on the arm of the chief.

"I should have known," Nathan mumbled.

"Perry, I'm glad I ran into you. Have you met Miss Dupont here? She's the private investigator that the Parkers hired to help you find their daughter's murderer," the chief said.

"We've met." He knew he should have walked her out.

"She will need full access to your files. Will you see that she gets a copy of everything you have?"

"Yes, sir," he reluctantly replied.

Mac looked at Nathan, smiling from ear to ear, tossing her hair with a flip of her head.

"I'm also going to see that she gets an office space here in the department so she has a place to work, and also be available, should you need her."

"Oh, Chief Cabot, you're so sweet to do that for me. Thank you," she said, pouring on the charm, and then winking at Nathan.

"Well, it's the least we can do for you to be so kind to help us on this," the chief said.

"Chief, we already have Detective Denzinger from the state police, in addition to Officer McCoy, assisting on this case. I really don't think we need any more help," Nathan said.

"Nonsense, a female perspective may be just what we need. Come my dear, let's see if we can find you an empty office," the chief said.

As they walked away from Nathan and Hank, Mac looked back, smiling and batting her eyes at them. "Damn her," Nathan swore under this breath.

"What's going on?" Hank asked.

"That, that woman. That's what's going on. I specifically told her that she could not have total access to my files. I would decide what information to give her. And, what did she do? She found the chief, flirted a little, and got exactly what she wanted." He marched to the break room to get his coffee, Hank at his heels.

"Are you actually mad about that, or jealous that you can't do something like that to get your way?"

Nathan stopped his coffee in mid-pour. He looked at Hank, squinting his eyes. "Do you really want to ask me that, considering the mood I'm in right now?"

"No, I guess not."

Nathan continued filling his cup, and then Hank poured himself one. Someone had left store-bought peanut butter cookies on the counter. Both men grabbed a couple, and headed back to Nathan's office.

"Hank, if you wouldn't mind, would you copy the Parker file for me?"

"Sure."

Before handing the file over to Hank, Nathan scribbled down a phone number from it. "While you do that, I'll take care of calling Isabella Osborne about coming down here for the interview."

"Sounds good. I'll be right back with the file," Hank said, leaving to do the copying.

Nathan dialed the number.

"Magick Potions and Gifts, how can I help you?"

"Hello, is this Miss Osborne?" He tapped a pencil against his desk.

"Yes, it is."

"Good. This is Detective Perry from the Mystic PD. I was hoping that you might be able to come down to the department this afternoon to discuss Ann Parker." He twisted his chair around to look out of the window.

"In the middle of the afternoon? I'm short-staffed as it is. I'd have to close the store."

"I realize you're an employee short, but this is very important for the investigation." He let out a deep breath. "I wouldn't want you to have to close your store during peak tourist time." He looked at his watch, and saw it was nine-thirty. "What if, instead, I came down there to do the interview after lunch?"

"I suppose that would work."

"Good. Thank you. I'll see you then."

As he turned his chair back around, and hung up the phone, he saw Gloria walking past his office. "Gloria, would you step in here, please?"

"Yes. What do you need?" she asked, coming back to the door.

"What makes you think I need something?"

She tilted her head, and frowned.

"Okay, I do need something. I hate being predictable. Could you take a copy of the Parker murder file to Mac Dupont later?"

"The lanky blonde who was hanging all over the chief's arm just a bit ago?"

"That's her. She was going to get a room at the Harbor House Hotel."

"And, why do you want me to take it to her? You, or Hank, can't do it?" She folded her arms in front of her.

"You saw how she was with the chief. I need a woman to take this to her hotel room, not a man."

Gloria burst into laughter. "I understand completely. Where's the file? I'll start copying it."

"Hank is doing that right now. I'll bring it up to you as soon as I make sure nothing is in it I don't want her to see," he said.

"Okay. I'll be waiting," she said, and left his doorway.

"What'd I miss?" Hank said, coming in with the file right after Gloria left. "Why was she laughing?"

"Nothing. You didn't miss anything. Did you get that file copied?"

"Yes, sir. Here it is." He handed both the original, and the copy, to Nathan.

He took the files, and began looking through the copied file, removing a few things.

Hank sat down. "Did you get a hold of that witch lady?"

"You mean, Miss Osborne. Yes, but she can't come down for an interview."

"Why?"

"It seems that Miss Parker was her only employee, and she refuses to close her shop to come down here. So, I'm going down there after lunch to talk to her," Nathan said.

"Do you want me to come along?"

"No, I need you to do some research on our latest victim. Can you start a background file on her? We need to be ready to take off running when we get the info from the state lab."

"I'll get started on that right away," Hank said. "Oh wait, I was going to see if you wanted me to deliver that file to Miss Dupont."

"No, Gloria's going to take it for me. If you went down there, I might not see you for days." Nathan tried not to laugh.

"Very funny. I'll start on the new file."

"And, I'm going to take this to Gloria." Both men got up and walked out.

Nathan headed down the hallway to the front desk. The image of Mac on the chief's arm still burned in his mind. *The chief isn't stupid. Why would he fall for her conniving trick?* "Gloria, here's the file for Miss Dupont. Before you take it to her, could you use the copy stamp on each page?"

"No problem."

"If you could deliver it this afternoon, I'd sure appreciate it."

"I'll take it right after lunch. It'll give me an excuse to eat out."

"Thanks." He walked back to his office, and spent the

rest of the day doing more online research about witches.

Right after noon, Nathan drove down to meet Isabella Osborne at her store. The first thing he noticed was the "Help Wanted" sign in the window. He entered the store, finding several customers inside. Isabella made eye contact, smiled, then turned back to the customer. He amused himself by wandering around the store looking at items. He lingered in the book section, where he found a book of spells.

"Did you find something you like?" Isabella asked, approaching a few minutes later.

She certainly dressed the part, again wearing a long black dress and light-colored makeup, with her eyes dark and mysterious.

"This book on spells has just about anything you can think of."

"Of course, and if you notice, most of them are not bad spells, but good ones. Let me show you." She moved in front of him. "Look, here is a spell to make someone fall in love with you, and here is one to help you lose weight."

"Those don't really work, do they?"

"They can, if you believe," she said.

"Do you believe?"

She hesitated at first. "Yes, I do believe. If I didn't, I wouldn't have this shop."

"You don't just do it for the tourists, and their money? I mean this is Mystic, Mass, and we get a lot of overflow tourists from Salem."

"I'd be lying if I didn't say that was part of it, but I do believe that you can have a spiritual experience with the right witchcraft."

"Did Ann Parker feel the same way?" Nathan asked.

Isabella turned and went to the back counter. Nathan followed her.

"Ann was skeptical when she first arrived here, but she came around to believe."

"When did she move here?"

"Eight or nine months ago."

"Did you hire her right away?"

"Yes, I hired her on the spot when she walked in holding the newspaper that had my 'Help Wanted' ad in it."

"The local newspaper?" Nathan asked.

"Yes."

He pulled out his small notebook, and began writing down some notes. "I notice that you have a 'Help Wanted' sign in the window this time. Why not place an ad in the paper again?"

"When I hired Ann, it was still cold weather. No tourists. With all of the people in town now, someone will see the sign, want the job, and stay in Mystic," she answered.

"Do you know anyone that would have wanted to murder Ann?"

"No. She was a wonderful girl. Everyone loved her."

"Who's everyone? She hadn't been in town long. Did she have many friends?"

Again, Isabella hesitated before answering, and Nathan made a mental note of that. "She met a lot of people from working here, and also at the different restaurants in town over lunch."

"Miss Osborne, are you a witch?" Nathan abruptly asked.

"I'm Wiccan."

"Did you bring Ann into your group?"

"She asked to join our coven. She visited, and yes, she eventually was asked to stay."

"Did she get along with everyone in the group, or did someone not like her, or not want her to join?" he asked.

"She got along well with everyone."

Nathan walked back over to the book section of the store and picked up a book about witches, bringing it over to the counter. "I want to buy this."

Isabella rang the transaction, taking Nathan's money.

"Make sure I get a receipt," he said.

"You're turning this in as an expense?"

"Research for the department. You never know, this might not be the only time we have a crime involving witchcraft."

She gave him his change, and the receipt. "I heard a body was found in the harbor."

"Yes, her name was Elizabeth Howe." He noticed a slight change in her expression. "Did you know her?"

"I did. She was a regular customer. What happened?"

"We don't know yet. Did Ann know her?" he asked.

"Maybe."

"Was Elizabeth a member of your group?"

Just as he asked that, some customers walked into the store. Isabella put his book into a bag, and handed it to him. "Have a nice day," she said to him, walking away to assist the customers.

Nathan drove back to the police department, and as he entered the building, he met Gloria leaving. "Late lunch?" he asked.

"Yes, and I have your file to deliver, too." She held up the folder. "Do you have a message for Miss Dupont?"

Boy, did he have a message for her, something like, *Go back to Boston, and I'll call you when I solve this.* "No, no message. I'm sure she'll find me when she needs to. The chief is setting up an office for her here in the department."

"As long as she understands that I don't work for her, I don't care where she works," Gloria said, continuing on her way.

Nathan stepped inside his office, where he found Hank working at the desk. "Have I been replaced?"

"Oh, no, sorry boss." Hank got up. "This was the quietest place I could find to work." He moved out of the way so Nathan could sit at his desk.

"What did you find out about Miss Howe?"

"Not much more than when I talked to her coworkers at the museum. I checked her finances, and she pretty much lived paycheck to paycheck. She had one credit card. It wasn't maxed out, but not much credit was left on it. I went out to her apartment, and spoke with the manager and a few neighbors. He said she kept to herself and rarely had any visitors. I tried to get him to let me into her apartment, but someone must have gotten to him. He said he needed a warrant before he'd let me in."

"Did he say when did she move there?" Nathan asked.

Hank thumbed through his notes. "She moved in about eight months ago."

"About the same time as Ann Parker. What about a previous address? You said the other day she lived here all of her life."

"I'm still working on that. The post office will get back to me on that, once they talk to the main office. How did the interview go with Miss Osborne?"

"She confirmed that Ann was interested in witchcraft, and Miss Osbourne introduced her to the coven. She was apprehensive with her answers. I think she knows more, but doesn't want to tell me. She did say that Ann knew Miss Howe from the store."

"What's your next step?" Hank asked.

"I want to talk to the Mr. Parker again, but I think I'll call him rather than drive up there." Nathan looked at his watch. "That's going to have to wait until tomorrow. I'm going to call it a day. You better get home, too. Your wife will be waiting at the door."

"You're probably right, but she's used to my odd hours," Hank said. He put his notebook into his pocket. "I'll get a warrant for Miss Howe's apartment tomorrow. Do you want to go with me to search it?"

"No. Take Mallory with you to log any evidence and keep me updated," Nathan said.

Hank got up, and left the office. Nathan checked the pink message slips on his desk. They could all wait until tomorrow. He was tired, and wanted a drink.

Nathan drove to his favorite bar, Capt's Waterfront Grill,

at the harbor. Inside, he took a seat at the bar.

"Hi, Nathan. Haven't seen you here in a while. What can I get you tonight?" bartender Scott Reid asked.

"Glenfiddich Scotch, neat."

"Coming right up," the bartender replied.

A few minutes later, a glass of scotch sat front of Nathan. "Long day at work?"

"Long week at work is more like it." He took a drink, enjoying the taste after a hard day. "Thanks, Scott."

"It's not hard to pour a drink. Want something from the grill?"

Nathan looked at the menu on the bar. "I'll take a fish sandwich and some fries."

While the bartender took the order to the cook, Nathan looked around the bar. Still too early for the regular evening crowd to come in, only a few people sat at tables. Probably tourists, Nathan thought. He spun back around to the bar, and took another sip of his drink. The television on the wall showed ESPN, where they were talking about the Patriots game coming up on Sunday.

"I can get you a couple tickets for that game, if you want." Mac Dupont slid onto the barstool next to him.

What the hell is she doing here, he thought. "What?"

"They're talking about the Pats game, and I thought you might like a couple tickets. I have two for the game this Sunday. Interested?"

"No." He turned back to his drink. Been there, done that, not again.

"No? You've got to be kidding. Two free tickets to the New England Patriots football game, and you're turning them down. Those are the hottest tickets around."

"Where did you get them?" he asked, without moving his head.

"I work for Mr. Parker, and he's affiliated with the Pats through his business. He always has tickets to give away."

The bartender walked up to Mac. "Can I get you

something to drink?"

"Margarita on ice, no salt, please."

"Good choice." He turned, and started working on her drink.

"So, again, why won't you take the tickets?" she asked Nathan.

"Because they are from Parker." He turned to face her. "I can't take something free from the father of a murder victim." He turned back toward the television.

"I'm sorry. I wasn't thinking."

Scott brought her drink, and placed it on the bar in front of her. She placed a twenty-dollar bill on the counter. "Tell me when I've used it all up," she said.

He took the money, and moved down the bar to help another customer.

"You weren't thinking. That's exactly why I don't want you working on this case with me. You weren't thinking," Nathan repeated.

Mac took a deep breath, and then a sip of her drink. "I would be a big help. You just don't realize it."

"Prove it," he said. Tipping the glass, the last drops of the honey-colored drink trickled down his throat.

"Let's sit at a table, and I will prove it to you."

"Fair enough." As he got up, he motioned to Scott to bring him another scotch. They walked over to an empty booth in the back corner of the bar. They both slid onto the seats opposite each other. "Okay, dazzle me."

"Ann Parker was not unemployed," she said.

"We know that. She worked at one of the shops in town."

"Well yes, but that wasn't her real job."

Scott approached with Nathan's drink, and also the food he'd ordered earlier. "Here you go, sir."

"Thanks," Nathan said. He turned to Mac. "Would you like something to eat? My treat."

"Sure, why not. I'll take one of those sandwiches and house salad. That sandwich looks good, and I'm starved."

"Here, take mine. Scott, bring me another sandwich, and I'll need another refill when the food is ready."

The bartender nodded, then walked back to the bar with the order. Mac continued her conversation, "As I was saying, working in town wasn't her actual job. She was really working for a guerilla newspaper in Boston."

"How do you know that?" he asked. "I thought she'd been gone from Foxborough for close to a year. How could she have had that information in her journal there?"

She took a drink of her margarita. "I read her emails."

"How did you read her emails? We have her laptop, and haven't cracked her password yet."

"The Parkers have their own server, and I was able to read her emails from before she moved out," Mac said.

"So, if she was working for a newspaper in Boston, what was she doing in Mystic?"

"That, I'm not sure of. Her emails were very cryptic. I plan on making a trip to visit her editor tomorrow. Would you care to go with me?" she asked.

Nathan wanted to know what Ann Parker was doing in Mystic for the newspaper. However, if he didn't go with her, could he trust Mac to give him all of the information she digs up in Boston? "Sure, I'll go with you. You might get more cooperation if a police officer is with you. It makes it more official," he said, sarcastically.

Mac laughed out loud. He wondered if that was the tequila working on her, or did she really think he said something funny.

"Actually, I think I'll get more cooperation if you don't identify yourself as the police."

"And, why is that?" he asked.

"Because they're a guerilla press. They don't like talking to cops."

He had to admit that she was probably right, but he wasn't about to let her know that. "We'll see. What time do you want to leave?"

"How does nine o'clock sound?"

"Sounds fine. Should I pick you up at your hotel?"

"You're going to pick me up?"

"This is a murder investigation, so why not let the police department pick up the tab for driving to Boston."

"Good point." She took another sip of her margarita, and Scott delivered Nathan's sandwich and third drink.

"Thanks, Scott," he said, before he went back to the bar. "Did you get the file I sent to you today?" He took a bite of his sandwich.

"Yes, I did. Thank you. I was a little surprised that you didn't bring it yourself."

"I was busy."

"When do I get the rest of it?" she asked.

Nathan took a sip of his drink and nearly choked. Between coughs, he said, "What do you mean, the rest of it?"

"The rest of the file. Come on, I was a cop long enough to spot holes in an investigation. You only sent me a partial file. Remember, what your chief said, I'm to get a copy of the whole file."

"The copy machine must be skipping pages again. I'll try to get you a full copy in the morning," he said.

"You know, Nathan, if I may call you that?"

He nodded his acceptance.

"I actually think we could work very well together, if you will just let me in."

He had to admit to himself that she seemed to know her stuff about investigating. "Okay, truce. I'll accept your help, if you will remember that this is my case, and I call the shots here."

"Agreed." She lifted her glass as if making a toast. Nathan did the same, clanging their drinks against each other, then taking a drink.

"You know, I'm getting a little tired, and I believe that tequila is beginning to work on me. I had better get back to my hotel," she said.

"Did you drive? We can't have you driving in Mystic in your condition," he joked.

"I walked," she answered.

"Well, in that case, you should allow one of Mystic's finest to walk you back to your hotel." He knew that sounded corny, but it was true. "How would it look if you were arrested for public intoxication?"

She smiled. "Let's go."

They both slid out of the booth, and paid their bill on their way out. "See you next time, Scott."

"Have a good evening, folks," Scott said.

Chapter Five

Monday dawned as a beautiful autumn morning in Mystic with a cool temperature and crisp air. Nathan entered the rear of the police department, taking two steps at a time, nearly knocking Gloria down as he went in.

"I'm sorry," he said, grabbing her by the shoulders to keep her from landing on the floor.

"I'm not." She laughed. "You sure seem like you're in a good mood today. What's up?"

"Nothing is up. It's such a nice morning and that makes me feel good," he said.

"Since when?" a male voice came from behind him.

Nathan turned. "Morning, Hank. Good weather always makes the day better."

Hank looked at Gloria, and just shook his head. "I don't believe him."

Nathan could only laugh.

"I'm going out to Miss Howe's apartment today to look for evidence, and talk to some of the neighbors. You sure you don't want to come with me?" he asked Nathan.

"Ah, no. I have to do some other stuff today. Gloria, could you copy Ann Parker's file for me?"

"Again?"

"Yes. Thanks." Nathan started back to his office with both officers following.

"I just copied that file yesterday. Why do you need it copied again today?" Hank asked.

"Some things didn't get included."

"Wasn't that the file I delivered to that lady PI yesterday?" Gloria asked.

"I copied every page in the file," Hank said.

They reached Nathan's office, and went in. He picked up the file, handing it to Gloria.

"Some of the pages didn't make it in," Nathan said. Gloria took the file, giving him a puzzled look. "All right, I took some things out of the file before I gave it to her, and she knew it. We've agreed to give a shot at working together on this case." He took a deep breath.

"I'm not surprised after the way she pranced around on Chief Cabot's arm yesterday. What did she do to convince you?

He paused, trying to decide how to answer.

"No, I don't want to know," Gloria said.

"You're kidding. Working together?" Hank said.

"Turns out she is a pretty good investigator. She found out that Miss Parker was really working on something for a cult-type newspaper in Boston."

"When exactly did you talk to her?" Hank asked.

Nathan sat down behind his desk. "Last night at Capt's. I stopped for a drink after work, and she showed up while I was there. We're driving to Boston today to talk the editor of that newspaper, to see if we can find out what Ann was here for."

"Now, I understand why you're in such a good mood." Gloria said.

"That's not why."

"I don't want to hear your explanation." She took the file and headed to the front.

"I need that file copied right away," he called after her. She waved back, but kept walking.

"Do you want me to come along? Maybe, as a chaperone?" Hank joked.

"No." Nathan could only shake his head. " I feel like I'm back in high school. I want you to continue working on Elizabeth Howe's case. We need to figure out how the two murders are related. Was she married?"

"No, single just like the Parker girl."

"Let me know if you find anything interesting." Nathan started gathering together a few items, pens, notebooks, and some of his business cards, to take with him. Hank left. Nathan sat down with his back to the door. He heard someone come in and assumed Hank had come back for something. "What do you want now?"

"I was hoping to ask you about your murder investigations."

Nathan recognized the voice immediately, and spun around in his chair. "Madam Mayor, I apologize. I thought you were Officer McCoy coming back in." He quickly stood.

"Sit down, Nathan. No need to apologize." They both sat down.

"What can I do for you?"

"I don't have to tell you how much I dislike having two murders in Mystic right now. It's the beginning of the fall tourist season. Our busiest time of the year, and it doesn't make us look very appealing as a vacation destination with two unsolved murders."

"I understand completely, ma'am, and I agree. We're working very hard to solve these crimes. Officer McCoy is heading out to the second victim's apartment right now. In a few minutes, I'm leaving for Boston to follow up on a lead on the first victim." He hoped the mayor picked up on the hint that he needed to leave.

"Well, I suppose I should let you go then. I just wanted to make sure you understood how important it is that these cases be wrapped up quickly."

"I understand more than you think, ma'am. Believe me, I take any murder seriously, and will do my very best to solve this," Nathan said.

"I'm glad to hear that, Nathan. Keep me informed of any progress. I suppose I better stop and see Chief Cabot while I'm here." The mayor stood up.

Nathan also stood. "Yes, ma'am. I will keep you updated." She walked out of the office, and Nathan looked at his watch. "Damn, I'm going to be late." He also wanted to leave before the chief came down to reiterate what the mayor said.

Gloria and Hank appeared back at Nathan's office door. "We waited until the mayor left. Here's the copied file again. Want me to take this one over to Miss Dupont, too?" she asked.

Nathan got up and took both files from her. He locked the original in a drawer and put the other on top of his desk. "No, I'll do that myself."

She laughed, and Hank could barely contain himself.

"All right. I know I'm the butt of your jokes right now. Go work," Nathan said.

Hank and Gloria left. Nathan grabbed the file that Gloria had copied, the other things he had put together, and ran out the door.

When he pulled up in front of The Harbor House, he saw Mac standing in front waiting for him. How could he miss her? She wore tight black jeans with black spike heels, and a tight, red pullover sweater. A long silver necklace hung around her neck, and she had a fancy backpack slung over her shoulder.

"You're late," she said, climbing into the car.

"I was detained by the mayor wanting an update on the murders. It's kind of hard to tell the mayor that you can't talk right now."

"I guess so."

"Didn't you have to deal with politicians when you were with the Boston PD?" he asked.

"No. I let the higher-ups handle that."

The drive to Boston only took about forty-five minutes, thanks to morning rush hour being over. Mac read off the address, and gave Nathan directions to the office of the *The*

Religare Affairs, a small weekly newspaper that published stories involving controversial topics.

"There it is, on the right. That's the building," she said.

Nathan found a parking garage two blocks past the building. They entered the offices a short time later.

"May I help you?" a young man said, sitting at the front desk in front of a wall partition. Behind it, the rest of the newspaper's office held seven desks, lots of old bookshelves filled full of stuff, and the smell of old musty books.

"We're here to see Michael Aldridge. My name is Mackenzie Dupont." She handed the man one of her business cards.

"Do you have an appointment?"

"No, we don't, but could you show him my card?" She flipped her hair back.

Nathan rolled his eyes. He knew she would do something like that.

The clerk got up, going to an office at the rear of the large room.

"You think just showing him your business card is going to get us in there?" Nathan asked.

"You'd be surprised the people that card will get me in to see."

The young man returned. "Mr. Aldridge said he can speak with you for a few minutes. Please follow me."

Mac looked at Nathan. "Told you."

They followed to the cramped office of the editor.

"I'm Michael Aldridge, please have a seat." They sat down.

"I'm Mackenzie Dupont. I'm a private investigator hired by William Parker to look into their daughter Ann Parker's murder. This is Nathan Perry."

"Why would you come see me about this?" Aldridge asked.

"Miss Parker worked for you."

"Miss Dupont, I'm sorry about the murder. I heard about

it on the news, but I don't know who Ann Parker is. Why would you think I did?" He nervously tapped his pen on the desk.

Nathan took a photo of Ann Parker and pushed it across the desk in front of the editor.

"I know she was a writer for you," Mac said. "I've read the emails you two sent back and forth to each other. There's no use denying it."

He dropped his pen on the desk. "Okay, I know her, and yes, she worked for me, but I hadn't heard from her in months. I assumed she quit. Now, I know different."

"What was she working on, Mr. Aldridge?"

"I'm rather busy. I can't help you. I think we're finished here." He rose from his chair.

Nathan had waited long enough. He took out his badge and held it in front of Aldridge's face. "I'm with the Mystic Police Department. You'll either answer our questions now, or you can answer them at the police department."

"You two need to leave. I have nothing more to say. I'm protected by the First Amendment. If you have any other questions, you'll have to discuss them with my attorney." He jotted a name on a piece of paper, handing it to Nathan. "Now, leave."

"You really think this little rag you call a newspaper falls under the First Amendment?" Nathan asked.

Mac took a deep breath and let it out slowly. "Mr. Aldridge, it's very likely Miss Parker was killed because of what she was working on for your paper. Don't you want the responsible party to be held accountable?"

"Please leave." He went to the door, and opened it.

They headed out the door, but Nathan stopped in front of Aldridge before stepping out. "We will be back, with a warrant."

"And, I'll have the Constitution to back me up."

They left the office, and Aldridge slammed the door behind them.

Mac was furious as they walked up the street to their

car. "You just couldn't keep it in your pants, could you?"

"What?"

"Your badge. You had to pull out your badge. I would have eventually gotten the information out of him, but no, you had to pull rank." She opened the car door, and got in.

Nathan got in the driver's side. "How would you have gotten the information, by flipping your hair a little more? That seems to be how you work."

"You know, it's a good thing you drove today."

"Why is that?"

"Because if I had driven, you'd be walking back to Mystic." She sat stoic, and stared straight out the windshield.

"As long as we're in Boston, do you mind if we stop by the medical examiner's office to see if they have the report finished on Elizabeth Howe?" Nathan asked.

"Sure, but you have to buy me lunch first," Mac said, yielding a little.

Nathan shook his head in disbelief. "Why do I have to buy your lunch?"

"You're the one with the expense account."

"I bet you have a bigger one with the Parkers," Nathan said.

She didn't answer.

Nathan put the car in gear and pulled out into traffic. "I know just the place."

Twenty minutes later, Nathan and Mac stood in front of Mama's Junkyard Dogs.

"You want to eat here?" Mac asked.

Nathan smiled. "What can I say? I love chili dogs. Come on." They got out and entered the establishment. In no time, they had their dogs, and opted to sit at a table out front on the sidewalk.

"It's going to take me days to get the editor of the paper to talk again," Mac said.

Nathan took a bite of his dog and swallowed. "I'll get a warrant. He'll talk, and give us what need then."

"You're crazy. You heard him. He's going to claim freedom of speech. It will take days in court, and no judge will make him talk. It would be a total waste of time. Let me work on him---alone."

Nathan just shook his head. "What kind of newspaper is *The Religare Affairs*? Their office reminded me of an underground type of paper." He took another bite of his chili dog.

Mac started to take a bite of her chili dog, but with one sniff, she dropped it back onto the basket. "You're partially right. It's a small start-up paper. They cover controversial political and religious topics."

He swallowed and took a drink of his soda. "What have they been writing about lately?"

Mac hesitated. "I don't know. I haven't read any of their recent issues."

"Maybe we should find out."

Mac looked down the street. "There's a newsstand down there. Maybe they carry the paper."

"Let's go check."

Mac stood.

"Aren't you going to eat your chili dog?" Nathan asked.

"I thought I could, but I just can't."

"But you didn't eat anything. At least have a few of my fries before we go." He held his basket of fries in front of her face.

She pushed his hand away. "You should know, I don't eat junk food."

He dropped the basket onto the table, and followed her down the sidewalk. "You're into health food?"

"Not necessarily health food, just healthy food, and now you know." She continued walking down the street until they reached the newsstand. "Hi, do you have *The Religare Affairs* paper?" she asked the man.

Nathan stood behind her, and the salesman handed her the paper as she gave him a dollar. "I'll take one too."

They both looked through the issue as they walked back to the car. "I don't see anything in here that could be written by Ann Parker," Mac said.

"Me either. Aldridge did say he hadn't heard from her in a few months. We need to see some back issues."

"They'll probably have some at the library." She folded the paper, and put inside her bag. "I'll go check there while you go to the medical examiner's office."

"You don't have a car."

"I'll take a cab." She stepped off the curb, and flagged one down. "Call me when you're finished. You can pick me up at the library." She got into the cab, and waved as she drove off.

Nathan drove to the ME's office. He was greeted by Dr. Philip Goode, Assistant Medical Examiner. He took Nathan to the morgue where he pulled Elizabeth Howe's body out of the refrigerated compartment.

Dr. Goode looked at the clipboard he was holding. "Elizabeth Howe, age twenty-six, cause of death was from a combination of a blow to the back of the head, and drowning." He showed Nathan the back of her head.

"I assume the head injury came first?" Nathan asked.

"Timewise, both happened pretty close together." He pushed the body back into the compartment. "Let's go to my office."

They entered Goode's office. "Coffee?"

"No, thanks," Nathan said. They sat. "If you had to guess, what do you think happened to Miss Howe?"

"Because of the defensive bruising on her arms, it's likely there was a struggle, so I'd say the blow to the head knocked her out, and then the body was dumped in the water. She'd probably been in water for about twenty-four hours before she was found."

"Did she have fresh water or salt water in her lungs?"

Goode looked through the autopsy report, which contained several pages. "Salt water."

"Sexual assault?"

"No."

"Did you find anything else?" Nathan asked.

"She had Valium in her blood," Goode replied.

"She was drugged?"

"Yes, most likely. It was probably put in her wine. It's the only thing we found in her stomach contents."

"No food at all?"

"None."

"What about Ann Parker? I don't recall seeing anything about drugs in her system," Nathan asked.

"Initially, drugs were not checked. After Valium was found in Miss Howe, we did run another tox screen and found it in Miss Parker's system also." He pulled something up on his computer. "Her stomach contents were fairly preserved. She's had spaghetti and wine twenty-four to forty-eight hours before death."

"The same wine as Miss Howe?"

"All we know is that both had drank red wine." Dr. Goode handed Nathan a file folder. "This is your copy of Miss Howe's autopsy report."

"Thanks."

****

While Nathan was at the medical examiners office, Mac was making progress at the library. She sat in the periodical section, looking through copies of *The Religare Affairs*. After reading numerous issues, she started printing several articles. Upon paying the library clerk for the copies, she went outside to call Nathan.

"Perry."

"It's Mac. I'm finished at the library. Can you come pick me up?"

"I can. I just finished here, and can be there in about twenty minutes."

"I'll be out front."

"Did you find anything?" he asked.

"Maybe. I'll explain when you get here."

After making the last turn, Nathan spotted Mac in front of the library, and stopped in front of her. Once she got in, he pulled back out into traffic for the drive back to Mystic.

"So, what did you learn from the medical examiner?" she asked.

"I got Elizabeth Howe's autopsy report. That's it on the seat."

Mac picked up the folder and read through it. "Wine, but no food in her stomach?" She thought for a few seconds. "What did Ann have in her stomach?"

"Spaghetti and wine."

"Was the wine the same as the Howe girl had?"

"Red wine is all they know. They also found Valium in both girl's blood."

"That's definitely a connection."

"What did you find at the library?" he asked.

"I think Ann was writing under a pen name at the paper."

"That kind of makes sense, if she didn't want her parents to find out where she was, or what she was doing. How did you figure that out?"

"It wasn't hard. I read enough of her emails to know her style."

"What was she writing about?" Nathan asked.

"The paper was doing a series on modern-day witches. I think those were her stories."

"Well, that would explain all the witchcraft stuff in her apartment. Her mother will be happy to know that she wasn't actually involved in witchcraft. What was the spin on the stories?"

"She became a member of a coven in the town," Mac said.

"Isabella Osborne already told me that."

"She never named the town in her articles. For all we

know, it could be Salem, but since you already have confirmed that, it's likely she was writing about your town."

They arrived in Mystic forty minutes later. He drove Mac to her hotel.

"I'll be at the police department in the morning," she said, getting out of the car, then leaning back in through the window. "Chief Cabot said my office will be ready by then. I'll make you copies of the newspaper articles for your file." She stepped away from the car, and walked into the hotel.

Nathan drove off, but needed to get gas. Before going to the police department, he turned into the gas station. He swiped his card at the pump, and started putting gas in the car.

Dana Tyler approached him. "Nathan, I need to talk to you."

"Hey, Dana. What's up?"

"I stopped by the police department to see you, but they said you were out."

"I've been gone all day."

"I was wondering if you had any updates on the murders?"

"The new girl getting a jump on you?" He finished with the gas, and hooked the nozzle back on the pump.

"No," she replied. A car pulled up behind Nathan's car.

"Get in my car, so I can move it."

She got in, and he pulled over next to where her car was parked. "Are these murders connected in some way?" she asked.

"I can't answer that right now."

"So, that's a 'No comment?'"

"That's a 'No comment.'"

Suddenly, someone knocked on Nathan's window, causing both he and Dana to jump. He lowered the window.

"Hi, Nathan. Hi, Dana. I'm not surprised to see you two together." It was Joe Cassidy, a local character who fancied himself a private investigator, and also attended high school with Nathan and Dana.

"Did you need something, Joe?" Nathan asked.

"I heard you have an out-of-town PI working with you on these murders. Why didn't you come to me, like last time, when you needed help?"

Nathan looked at Dana, who was giving him an evil eye. He looked back at Joe. "I can't really comment on that, Joe. You understand."

"Oh, right." He looked at Dana, and whispered, "Not in front of the press."

Nathan didn't say anything.

"I better let you two get back to your conversation. I'll talk with you later, Nathan. Have a nice day." Joe walked away.

"What's this about a PI helping with your investigation?" Dana asked.

"I don't know how Joe knew about that. This is off the record, okay?"

"If Joe knows about it, it should be fair game, right?"

She has a point, he thought. "Ann Parker's parents hired her to look into the murder."

"Her? The PI is a woman?"

Nathan clinched his eyes shut. "Yes, she's a woman."

Dana opened the car door to get out.

"Dana, wait." He got out also, catching up to her at her car. "What are you mad about?"

"I'm not mad, but I don't like it when you withhold things from me. Now, I have a lot of work to do."

"But, that's my job. I can't tell you everything about the case."

She got into her car to leave, but rolled down the window. "Don't forget to call me for dinner." She backed her car out and drove off.

He closed his eyes, took a deep breath, then let it out, opening his eyes. "I will never figure women out."

Back at the police department, Nathan saw Hank sitting with Gloria in the break room. He joined them, placing his portfolio on the table.

"How was Boston?" Hank asked.

"More important, how was Miss Dupont?" Gloria added, snickering.

"Boston was promising, and Miss Dupont is a top-rate investigator, but I'll deny ever saying that."

"What did you find out?" Hank asked.

"It appears that Ann Parker wrote under a pen name for a small newspaper in Boston. She was working on a series about witchcraft in a Massachusetts town."

"Mystic?" Gloria asked.

"She didn't name the town in her articles, but I'm sure of it."

Gloria looked at his portfolio. "You've not been to your office yet, have you?"

"No. Why?"

"Mallory needed to see you. I told her to slip a note under your door. If you came in, you might not check your messages, but would probably find that note."

He looked at his watch. It was late in the day. "Hopefully, she's not left yet." Nathan went to his office, unlocked the door, and found the note on the floor. After reading it, he headed to Mallory's office, and found her at her desk.

She looked up. "Hi, Nathan. You got my note?"

"Yes. What did you find?"

Mallory walked over to unlock the gate door, letting him in. He sat across the desk from her.

"I finally broke into Ann Parker's phone that we found at her apartment. I think she had a boyfriend here in Mystic."

"What makes you think that?" he asked.

"I found several emails on the phone between Ann and a man."

"Who is he?"

"I don't know. She never addressed him by name, and he used one of those free email web sites, Gem underscore man at dayrep dot com, no name was attached to his emails."

"Interesting. Anything else?"

"From the content of the emails, it seems like he's local. He mentioned several places in Mystic for them to meet. I printed them for you." She handed him a stack of papers.

"This is a big help. Thank you." He started to leave, but turned back to her. "Did you ever hear about the grant to build a lab for you?"

"Nothing yet," she replied. "Hopefully, soon."

Back in his office, Nathan put the copies of the emails in a folder, and then into his briefcase to take home to read. After locking his office, he left for the day.

****

On his way to work the next morning, Nathan stopped to talk to Isabella Osborne at her store. He arrived just as she was unlocking the door.

"Miss Osborne, would you mind if I took a few moments of your time?" He followed her into the store.

"Is this about Ann?" She turned the lights on, and walked behind the counter.

"It is."

She then went to the office to leave her coat and bag. Nathan waited for her to come back out. She stepped behind the counter, and he stood in front of her. She put the money for the day into the cash register.

"Do you know who Ann was dating here in Mystic?"

"What makes you think she was seeing someone?"

"Miss Osborne, I'm trying to find out who murdered your employee. I'm asking for your help with these questions."

Isabella stopped what she was doing, closing the cash register. "I'm sorry. I really don't know if she was seeing anyone. She never mentioned it. What makes you think she was?"

"She was attractive. I can't imagine her staying home alone every night."

"Detective, I really want to help, but I just don't know." Two tourists came into the store. Isabella went to assist them while Nathan browsed.

After the customers paid for their items, Nathan came back to the counter. "What about at the coven meetings? Did she ever spend time with any of the men there?"

"I never noticed her hanging around with anyone in particular."

"Is fraternizing between members allowed?" he asked.

She stopped what she was doing. "It's not the military. Of course, its allowed. I just never noticed." She brought out a box of t-shirts, and began folding them.

Nathan took out his notebook. "Could you give me the names of the other people in the coven? I'd like to talk to them too."

Isabella laughed. "Most of those people don't want anyone knowing what they're involved in. I can't violate their trust."

"How many people are in the group?"

"No more than thirteen."

He wrote that down. "From my research, I understand the leaders are the High Priest and High Priestess. Can you at least tell me who they are?" He wrote both titles down in his notebook, waiting for her to answer.

But she didn't answer.

"Miss Osborne?"

He startled her. "I can't. I'm sorry. I think you should leave."

"One more thing, could I see her personnel file?"

"Why?"

"I need to collect her personal information, a copy of her job application, banking information, things like that."

"I suppose I could do that." She stepped through a curtain to the back of the store, and came back out a few minutes later. "I don't have time to copy it, could you do that and return the original to me?"

"That will be no problem. Thank you." He didn't want to push her with any more questions. Maybe at another time, he could get her to talk more. "Please call me, if you decide to talk about the coven." He gave her his card and then left.

Once he got to his office, he unlocked the door, checked in at the front desk to get any messages, and with the dispatcher. Back in his office, he sat down, took the case file out of his briefcase, and then read his email. After about an hour of work, Nathan started yawning, and realized he didn't have his usual morning coffee. He grabbed his cup, heading to the break room.

He found Hank at the coffeemaker filling his cup. "Morning. Let me fill that for you," he said.

"Thanks." Nathan held out his cup while Hank poured the coffee. "If you have time, I need to be updated on what you found at Elizabeth Howe's apartment."

Hank finished pouring, and put the coffee pot back. "I can, but you need to know something first. Chief Cabot put Mac Dupont in an office here this morning."

"I knew she was supposed to be here today. Where's her office?" He took a drink of his coffee.

"Down the hall, last door on the left."

"I need to talk to her. I'll meet you in my office in a few minutes to go over what you found yesterday."

Hank went to Nathan's office, while Nathan walked down the hall. He found Mac sitting at her desk. "I always wondered what was behind this door. Now, I know. It's a closet." He entered the very small room, and sat down, putting his coffee on her desk.

"It still has that cleaning fluid, disinfectant, smell lingering," Mac said. "I'm glad you're here. I was going to look for you later. I have something."

"What's that?"

"Mr. Parker said you wanted to know about David Anders."

"Ann's former boyfriend. You found something?"

"I didn't find anything suspicious, yet. He's a bartender at a pub in Foxborough." She took two pages off of her printer, handing them to Nathan.

He quickly read through them. "He's got a few traffic tickets, an old pot possession charge of less than two ounces, and one DUI where he was barely over the legal limit. This is interesting; he was arrested for assault on an earlier girlfriend."

"I doubt the Parkers knew that, but they didn't really like him anyway."

"Why didn't they like him?" Nathan asked.

"They didn't think he was good enough for their daughter, and tried to get Ann to break up with him."

"Is that why they stopped seeing each other?"

"The Parkers didn't know."

"We need to talk to Anders," Nathan said.

"We need to talk to Anders," Mac repeated.

"I'll call him, to see if we can pay a visit." He held up the pages on Anders. "Thanks for this." Picking up his coffee cup, he headed back to his office.

Nathan forgot Hank was waiting in his office. "I need to make a call. Can we go over your info on Miss Howe later?" he asked.

"Sure. It can keep." Hank left the office.

Nathan dialed a number. "Can I speak to David Anders?"

"This is David."

He could tell he had woken Anders up. "Mr. Anders, this is Nathan Perry, from the Mystic Police Department. I need to talk to you about Ann Parker."

"Yeah, so what about her?"

"What about her? Really?" He couldn't believe this guy's attitude. "I'm investigating her murder, and need to talk to you."

"Murder? What? Ann's dead?" Anders sounded panicked.

"You didn't know?"

"What happened?" Anders asked, sounding more coherent now.

"Would you be willing to answer a few questions tomorrow morning at your apartment?"

"What kind of questions?"

"Just routine stuff. We need to know more about Ann," Nathan said.

"I guess so. What time?"

"Can I come around noon?"

"Sure. Can you tell me what happened to her?"

"Look it up online." Nathan hung up.

Chapter Six

Wednesday morning, Nathan stopped at The Witch's Brew for breakfast. He sat at his usual booth by the window, near the counter. He waved to Ginger as he took his seat, and placed his morning newspaper on the table, picking up the menu.

"Good morning," Ginger said, walking up to the table. She put a cup in front of him, filling it with coffee. "How's everything with you this morning?"

"So far, so good, but I've not been to work yet."

"What do you have planned for your son for Halloween?"

"It's a little hard to plan something when he's in D.C. and I'm here." He took a drink of coffee.

"Halloween is a special time for kids. You better come up with something, even if you're here. Got any new pictures?" she asked.

Nathan showed her some photos on his phone.

"He's sure getting big."

"He's doing great. I just wish I could see him more often. He's grows so much between my visits."

Ginger handed the phone back to him. "He's the spitting image of you."

Hank walked up, and slid onto the opposite side of the booth from Nathan. "Morning," he greeted, taking a menu. "You missed roll call."

"I called in that I'd be late."

"What can I get you boys?" Ginger asked.

"I want pancakes with a side of bacon," Nathan said.

"I'll take the same with some coffee, and a glass of milk." Hank put the menu back into the holder.

"Coming right up." Ginger headed to the kitchen.

"I'm sorry I didn't get to your report about Miss Howe's apartment yesterday. Want to give me an abridged version now?"

Ginger approached the table with a cup and coffee pot. She filled the cup for Hank and topped off Nathan's.

"Thanks," they both said. Ginger left to attend to the other tables.

"I emailed you the list of what I found at Miss Howe's apartment," Hank said. "It was almost identical to what we found at Ann Parker's place. This apartment was even in the same building."

"Did you find a computer?"

"No, no computer. Mallory has her cell phone though. There's one other thing. The landlord said her car wasn't there, and hadn't been for several days."

"Did you put out a bulletin on it?"

"Yes. I had to check with the BMV to get the information on it first."

"Good."

The waitress came to their table with their food and placed it in front of them. "Can I get you anything else?"

"I think we're good. Thanks."

Hank poured some syrup on his pancakes. "Ann Parker's car hasn't been found yet either."

"I know, and that bothers me. Those cars could be anywhere. This case really has me baffled." Nathan took the syrup from Hank, covering his pancakes, cut a bite, then swallowed.

"A chop shop could have them stripped by now," Hank suggested.

"I thought of that, but it doesn't go with the way they were murdered. This all has to do with the witch thing. I'm sure of it."

Hank chewed his bite of bacon, and swallowed. "You know there's several witch museums over in Salem. Maybe we could talk to them about any activity in the area."

"That's a good idea. No one around here seems to want to talk to us. Could you check on that?"

"I'd be glad to."

"Gentlemen, how are your pancakes?" Ginger asked, stopping by the table, still holding the coffee pot, albeit with a little less coffee in it.

"Perfect, as always," Hank said, then drained the last of his milk.

"I agree." Nathan took the last drink of his coffee.

"Good. If you don't need anything else, I'll get your checks."

"I need a large coffee to go," Nathan said.

Ginger looked at Hank. "Does he drink coffee all day at work?"

Hank chuckled. "He does."

"How do you sleep with all that caffeine in you?" she asked Nathan, as he got up.

"I sleep very well, thank you." He and Hank followed Ginger to the counter to pay their bills, and get Nathan's coffee.

At the police department, Nathan headed to Mac Dupont's office. He stepped around the door, and started to say something, then realized she wasn't alone.

"Hey, hello, Nathan."

"Joe? What are you doing here?"

"You two know each other?" Mac asked.

"We sure do," Joe said. "Nathan and I went to high school together. He also asks me for help whenever he get stuck on a case, right Nathan?"

"Something like that." When Joe turned away, Nathan

shook his head. Mac tried to keep from laughing.

Joe turned back to Nathan. "I talked to Chief Cabot to volunteer my services again with your murder case. He sent me to see Miss Dupont."

"We appreciate that, Joe. Right now, I need talk to Mac about something, privately. We'll call you, if we need anything."

"They call you Mac? How cool is that?" Joe said, standing up.

Nathan stepped out of the doorway, so Joe could leave.

"You're sure you'll call?" Joe asked.

"If we need help, you'll be my first call."

Joe left the office. Mac started to speak, but Nathan held up his hand for her to stop. He watched down the hall until Joe rounded the corner, out of sight and ear shot. "I think he's gone."

"Thank God, you came when you did," Mac said. "He had me trapped in here."

Nathan stood at the door to keep a watch in case Joe came back. "Basically, he's harmless."

"He's creepy!"

"He's that too." Nathan laughed. "I'm getting ready to leave to see David Anders. Want to go with me?"

"I do." She got up and grabbed her coat.

An hour later, they were at the door of David Anders' apartment in Foxborough. Nathan knocked.

The door opened. "Yeah." The man standing there was around six-foot, medium build, messy brown hair, and brown eyes. It looked like he hadn't shaved in a couple days.

"David Anders?" Nathan asked.

"Yes."

Nathan showed his badge. "I'm Nathan Perry, from the Mystic Police Department. I spoke with you on the phone yesterday about Ann Parker."

"Ah, yeah, sure. Come in." He opened the door wider to let them in.

Nathan stepped in first. The apartment was a mess, with very little furniture. A futon, that was covered with wadded-up clothes, looked like it doubled as the couch.

"Let me clean that off," Anders said. He quickly picked up the clothes and tossed them into a corner of the room. "My roommates don't clean much. They work days, and sleep at night. I work nights, and usually sleep all day. Please, sit down."

Nathan and Mac sat on the futon. He took his notebook and pen out. "This is Mac Dupont. She's consulting on the case."

"Can I get you something to drink?"

Nathan looked around the room. Old pizza boxes and beer cans were tossed about on the floor. "No, nothing. Thanks."

"Nothing for me either," Mac added.

Anders sat on a nearby chair. "I looked online about Ann's murder. I can't believe she's dead. Who do you think did it?"

Nathan and Mac looked at each other. "We don't know yet."

"I cared a lot about her."

"Let's start from the beginning. How did you and Ann meet?" Nathan asked.

"She was a regular at the bar where I work. We struck up a friendship, then after a few weeks, I asked her out. She said, 'Yes.'"

"When was that?" Mac asked.

"About a year ago, I guess. We saw each other pretty regularly for a few months. Then, she asked me to her home for Thanksgiving dinner with her family. I should've never gone."

Nathan wrote down some notes. "What happened at Thanksgiving?"

"We didn't even get to dinner," Anders said. "When her father found out I was just a bartender, he made it very clear to me that I wasn't good enough for his daughter. He and Ann argued." He paused for a few seconds. "I don't think I ever fought with my old man as bad as they were going at it."

"What did he say to her?" Nathan asked.

"He told her a bartender wasn't the right type of man for her. She should be seeing someone with more intelligence, and a career, like a doctor or lawyer. That's when I got pissed. I told the old man off, and left."

"What about Ann? Did she go with you?" Mac asked.

Anders ran his fingers though his hair, sitting back in the chair. "I waited in my car for about fifteen minutes. She never came out, so I drove home."

Nathan took more notes.

"When did you see Ann again?" Mac asked.

Anders thought for a few seconds. "She showed up at the bar the following Saturday night."

"How'd that go?" Nathan asked.

"Not as well as Ann thought it would. She was all apologetic, acting like everything was okay."

"But it wasn't?" Mac asked.

"Hell no, it wasn't. She should have left with me that day. You know what she said she did? She said she had dinner with them. I broke things off with her right then. All she cared about was being able to get that trust fund of hers."

"Did you see her after that night?" Nathan asked.

"She came into the bar a few times the following week. She left with a different guy each night, and made sure I saw her leave with them."

"That must have made you mad."

"It did. Those guys weren't any better than me."

"Did you confront her about it?" Mac asked.

"No. I was done with her. I moved on," Anders said.

"Do you know of anyone that would want to hurt her? Anyone that didn't like her?" Nathan asked.

"No, no one." Anders shifted in his chair.

"Come on, David," Mac prodded. "No one was ever

jealous of her money? Her privileged life? Maybe someone in her inner circle of friends?"

"Her friends loved her. They were all just as privileged as she was. Spoiled brats, if you ask me. If any of them were jealous, they didn't show it," he replied.

Nathan decided to change directions with the questioning. "Did you know she was interested in witchcraft?"

"Witchcraft? No way. Ann's Catholic, her uncle's a priest."

Nathan stopped writing, and looked up at Anders. "What's the uncle's name?"

I'm not sure. It's her mom's brother. He was there on Thanksgiving. She said he lived in their pool house."

"You said you read about the murder online after I spoke with you on the phone. Where were you the night she was murdered?" Nathan asked.

Anders stood. "You think I killed her?"

"Calm down, David," Mac said. "It's just something we have to ask."

"We need to rule you out," Nathan added.

"I didn't kill her."

"David, you were arrested once for hitting a past girlfriend. Did you ever get so mad at Ann that you hit her?" Mac asked.

He stood, walking to the window. "I never hit Lisa, my old girlfriend. It was her word against mine, and the judge believed her." He turned back toward them. "I never laid a hand on Ann, and I didn't kill her."

"Where were you that night?" Nathan asked again.

"I don't have an alibi, if that's what you're getting at. It was my night off. I was home alone." He sat back down.

"Where were your roommates?" Mac asked. "I thought you said they worked days, and were home at night."

"They were out partying, and I was in my room sleeping when they got home."

"We're going to need your roommates' names, and phone numbers." Mac handed Anders a notepad and pen.

He wrote down the information, and handed it back.

"We also need the names of Ann's friends in Foxborough," Nathan added.

Anders finally finished the list, handing it back to Mac.

"I think we have what we need." Nathan stood. "If we think of anything else, would it be okay if we came back to talk to you?"

"I guess," Anders replied.

"Thanks for talking to us," Mac said as they walked out the door. She and Nathan headed to the car. "What do you think?"

"I want to believe he didn't do it, but with no alibi, I can't rule him out."

"So, what now?" Do we head back to Mystic?"

"Actually, I want to talk to the Parkers again, while I'm here."

They reached their car. "Great. Let's go."

"I'd really like to talk to them without you with me. Is there someplace I can drop you to wait for me? It shouldn't be long," Nathan said.

"You don't want me to go with you?"

They got into the car. "I think it would be better if I talked to them myself."

"What are you going to ask them?"

"I want to hear their version of Thanksgiving. If you're there, I think they will look to you for guidance with their answers."

Mac let out a deep breath. "There's a coffee shop near their home. I can wait for you there."

With Mac's directions, Nathan found the coffee shop. He stopped in front, letting her out. "I'll call you when I leave the Parkers' home."

"I'll be here."

Nathan drove off. A few minutes later, he was at the Parkers' front door. Just like last time, Patrick led him to the same room to wait.

"Mr. and Mrs. Parker will be right with you."

Nothing had changed since the last time he was there, other than there were fresh flower arrangements on every table now. An easel held a large photo of Ann, all likely from the funeral.

William Parker entered the room. "Detective Perry, I wasn't expecting you. Have you found out who murdered my daughter?"

"No, sir. Not yet. I have a few more questions to ask you."

"You should have called." Mr. Parker sat down.

"I was in Foxborough. I hope you don't mind me stopping by."

"I suppose not, if it will help, but in the future, it would be nice to be notified ahead of time."

"William, Patrick said that detective is here." Mrs. Parker entered the room, followed by a priest.

Nathan stood.

"Oh, you're here," she said.

"Yes, ma'am. How are you?" Nathan asked.

"How do you think I am? I buried my only child yesterday." She circled the room, touching and smelling several of the flower arrangements, stopping momentarily to gaze at Ann's photo.

Nathan noticed she was holding onto her cross necklace again.

"Margaret, come sit down," the priest said.

She walked over to the couch, and sat next to her husband. "Detective, this is Father Michael, my stepbrother."

"It's nice to meet you, Father. I'm Detective Perry." Nathan sat back down.

"Yes, Margaret mentioned you were trying to find poor Ann's killer. How is that going?"

"We're working on it every day," Nathan answered. " Mr. Parker, when we spoke last time, you failed to mention that David Anders was here with Ann for Thanksgiving dinner, and you also didn't mention that Father Michael was here also."

"I didn't think it was important, and to be honest, you didn't ask."

"I'm asking now. Tell me about Thanksgiving."

"You're being very rude, Detective," Mrs. Parker said.

Nathan took a deep breath before responding. "Mrs. Parker, I apologize. I'm trying to find out who killed your daughter. Withholding any information, no matter how irrelevant you, or your husband, think it may be, can hamper the investigation."

"I see. William, answer his questions," she instructed her husband.

"He's not really asked me anything yet, dear."

Nathan was getting a headache. "Mr. Parker, again, would you tell me about Thanksgiving?"

"I don't think there's much to tell. She brought that bartender home for dinner. He realized that he was out of his class, and left."

Nathan took out his notebook. "You and your wife were there, and Father Michael also?"

"Yes, I was," the priest said. "I always come to Thanksgiving and Christmas dinners. They're my only family," he said, motioning toward the Parkers.

Nathan looked at Mr. Parker. Tell me about the argument you had with Ann that day."

"Argument? We didn't have any argument," Mr. Parker said. "Why do you think we argued?"

Nathan didn't want the Parkers to know he had talked to Anders, although they may have figured that out already. "Well, you indicated you didn't see Ann much after Thanksgiving. I just assumed there had been some sort of disagreement between you two."

"You assumed incorrectly," Mr. Parker said, standing. "I think you should leave, Detective. Come, Margaret." He took his wife's hand to help her stand, and they left the room.

"Let me walk you out, Detective," Father Michael said.

Nathan put his notebook away, and followed the priest

outside.

"You have to understand that Margaret and William are still in mourning. Ann's funeral was yesterday. They only have each other now."

"And you," Nathan said. "There's still you."

"Not really. I'm Margaret's stepbrother. Although, we did grow up together as true brother and sister. Margaret's mother passed away when she was young. My father had also passed away. Our parents met each other at church, and eventually got married."

"Obviously, the church is important to your family."

"How so?"

"I've noticed every time Mrs. Parker becomes upset; she grasps her cross necklace. And you, well, you became a priest."

"Oh, of course."

"What parish are you with?"

"I retired a few years ago. It was time for the younger priests to take over. I live in Margaret's guest house now, and fill in at any of the churches that need a substitute to minister to the flock."

"What happened at Thanksgiving, Father?" Nathan asked.

"It was-- it was just as William said."

"Thank you, Father. I should be going." Nathan was skeptical about Father Michael's answer, but this wasn't the time or place to challenge him on it. He opened the door to his car.

"God be with you, son," Father Michael said, making the sign of the cross in front of him.

Nathan smiled. "Thank you, Father." As he drove down the driveway, he called Mac. "I'm on my way to get you."

"How'd it go?" she asked.

"I've got conflicting versions of what happened on Thanksgiving. I'll be there in a few minutes."

After picking up Mac, he explained everything he

learned from the Parkers. When they arrived back in Mystic, they went straight to the police department.

Nathan unlocked his office door. He and Mac stepped inside.

"So, what's next?" Mac asked, sitting down.

"It's about time you got back." Gloria stepped into the office, then looked at Mac. "Oh, I'm sorry. I didn't realize Miss Dupont was with you."

"That's okay, Gloria, is it?" Mac asked.

"Yes, ma'am. Officer Gloria Wheeler."

"You can call me Mac, Gloria."

Gloria nodded.

"We just returned. Anything go on today?" Nathan asked.

"The Historical Society Museum where Miss Howe worked, called. They cleaned out her desk, and wanted to know what to do with her personal effects. I asked Hank to pick them up."

"Good. Is he around?"

"His shift ended about thirty minutes ago. He's left for the day. He gave the effects to Mallory to log as evidence until we can release them to Miss Howe's brother." Nathan started to say something, but Gloria stopped him by holding up her hand. "Mallory's left for the day too."

"Thank you. Anything else?"

"You had a few phone calls, but nothing urgent. They're in your slot, up front. Dana Tyler stopped by to talk to you. She asked that you call her as soon as you got back."

Nathan looked at his watch. "I'll call her in the morning."

"She sounded like it was pretty important."

"It always is."

Gloria turned to leave. "It's your ass."

"What?"

"I said, I'm going home too." She left.

Chapter Seven

With the Halloween month of October just two days away, the town was bustling with activity. Even early on a Thursday morning, The Witch's Brew was near capacity. Nathan stood at the door to see if his breakfast companion had already arrived. Finally, he spotted her sitting in a booth about halfway down the room. She waved, as he walked to join her.

"Morning, Mac, " he said, sliding onto the bench seat across from her. A waitress brought a coffee pot, and filled the cup in front of him. Mac already had her food. "Could you bring me a number one?"

"Sure will." Before the waitress left, she filled Mac's coffee cup also.

"Did you get some rest last night?" Mac asked.

"Some. I kept going over what Anders and the Parkers said about Thanksgiving."

"I was thinking about the same thing. I came up with an idea. Who haven't we talked to yet that was there on Thanksgiving?"

"I don't know." He took a drink of coffee.

"The staff."

"They make their staff work on a holiday?" he asked.

"Yes."

"Interviewing the staff is brilliant."

"I do have my moments." Mac winked.

After a short time, Ginger brought Nathan's food. "I never know who you'll be with next," she said.

Nathan laughed. "This is Mac Dupont. She's helping with the murder investigation."

Ginger leaned down to whisper to Nathan. "As much as I love seeing you in here, you should have gone somewhere else this morning." She stood back up.

"Why?" Nathan asked. Before Ginger could say anything, he saw why.

Ginger stepped away as Dana Tyler walked up with a young lady following her.

"Dana, good morning," Nathan said. He didn't know why, but he felt like he was just caught with his hand in the cookie jar.

"Good morning," Dana replied, then looked at Mac.

"Dana, this is Mac Dupont. She's a private investigator consulting with us on the recent murders. Mac, this is Dana Tyler, reporter for the *Mystic Messenger* newspaper."

Mac dabbed at the corner of her mouth with a napkin. "It's nice to meet you. I've read some of your stories. They're very good."

"Thank you," she answered with an awkward smile. "This is Emily Haskell. She's the new reporter the paper recently hired."

"Welcome to Mystic," Nathan said. She looked young, but attractive. He could see why Dana felt a little threatened by her.

"Thank you," Emily replied.

Dana looked at Nathan. "Did Gloria tell you I wanted you to call me when you got back in town yesterday?"

"She did, but I was busy. I thought I'd call you today when I got to work. What did you need?"

"I wanted to ask you to my house for dinner last night."

"Oh. Sorry." He tried to smooth it over with a smile, but it wasn't working.

Without saying another word, Dana marched out of the café with Emily following her like a puppy.

"Girlfriend?" Mac asked.

"Not exactly. I really don't want to discuss it." Losing his appetite, he pushed his plate of food away. "Back to the Parkers' staff. Who would have been working on Thanksgiving? Surely, not the whole staff?"

"No. I'd guess the butler, cook, and one maid, who would be helping in the kitchen, as well as serving."

"So, three to interview."

"Yes, and the interviews need to be done separately, but at the same time. We don't want them warning each other, or for the Parkers to coach them," Mac said.

"Good point."

"I was there on a Saturday once. There was no staff there that day."

"I hate waiting until Saturday. What about a weekday? How late do they work?"

The waitress dropped off their checks as she walked by.

"I'm not sure. I've never been there late on a weekday. I'd say the kitchen staff would leave once they finish cleaning after dinner. The butler, maybe around the same time."

"Can you get the names and addresses of the staff we need to talk to?" he asked.

"I just need to get to my computer."

Nathan and Mac left money on the table to cover their bill, plus tip. Then, they left for the police department.

Nathan was reading his email and phone messages when Mac walked into the office. She sat down, and handed him a sheet of paper.

"What's this?" he asked.

"The names and addresses of the butler, maid, and cook."

"Excellent. I got approval for overtime for Hank and Gloria to help us with the interviews tonight, so we can see everyone at the same time."

"What time will that be?" she asked.

"We'll all meet here at six-o'clock. By the time we drive to Foxborough, and find their homes, hopefully they'll be home."

"Great. See you at six."

"Oh, wait," he said. "Would you be able to get a list of the people that were at the funeral home for Ann's viewing, and also to the funeral?"

"I'll see what I can do."

"Thanks. I'd like to see who attended."

"I'll let you know." Mac left his office.

Around one-o'clock, Nathan realized he hadn't eaten lunch. He walked into the break room to see what he could find in the machines. He ended up with a protein bar and a soda. Just as he was walking back to his office, he heard Hank.

"Hey, got a minute?"

"Sure. Come in."

Hank walked in and sat down. "I picked up Elizabeth Howe's personal effects from her employer yesterday. I had Mallory log them in, to keep until we can release them to her brother."

"Was there anything interesting?" Nathan also sat down, then took a bite of the protein bar, and opened the can of soda.

"There was a date book. I looked through it. She used a lot of abbreviations to note meetings or events. I asked Mallory to see if she could figure out what they mean."

"I should probably check in with her about what she has on the case." Nathan took a drink of his soda.

"I need to get back on patrol. See you at six," Hank said, leaving the office.

Nathan followed him out, but turned toward the front of the building where Mallory's office was located.

He stepped through the doorway of her office, and was surprised to see changes in the Evidence Room. "What happened in here?" Instead of finding her at the desk locked in the cage, she was at a desk just inside the door.

"Hi, Nathan. I decided I needed to separate my evidence job from my I.T. job," Mallory said.

"I like it." He sat down next to her desk. "Hank said he brought Elizabeth Howe's date book to you. Were you able to decipher any of it?"

"Not yet, but the same initials fall on the same dates every month, so I'm thinking they must indicate some sort of meeting. I'm going through some of the books from her apartment to see if they might be the key for the code."

"Good. My second question is, have you made any progress on Ann Parker's cell phone to identify who she was dating in Mystic?"

"Not really. I went through all of her emails. I can tell you when and where they went on dates, but she never addresses him by his name. Other than emailing him at the address we have, I don't know how to find him."

"Right now, he's a suspect. I don't want to email him and take a chance on him taking off before we can identify him."

"I hadn't thought of that."

"We'll use that idea as a last resort. Until then, can you email me the dates and addresses of the places Ann and our mystery man went? It looks like we're going to have to do some old-fashion police work, and visit the places. Maybe someone will remember them."

"I'll get that to you right away," she said.

"There's no big rush. I probably won't get to it until tomorrow, or Monday. Thanks." Needing to prepare for the interviews later than night, he walked back to his office.

At six-o'clock sharp, Gloria and Hank both entered Nathan's office. "We're not late, are we?" Gloria asked.

"No. Mac hasn't got here yet. Have a seat. Thanks for working late to help with this. I hope your spouses don't mind."

"My husband doesn't mind. It's still high school football season. He works late every night," Gloria said.

"My wife is used to my late hours," Hank added.

Mac walked in. "I'm sorry I'm late."

"You're not, but we do need to get started." Nathan waited until Mac sat down to begin. "Now, that we're all here, I'll fill you in on exactly what we're doing. As you know, Mac and I interviewed Ann Parker's former boyfriend, David Anders, yesterday. Afterward, I spoke with Mr. and Mrs. Parker, as well as Mrs. Parker's stepbrother. The family gave a different version of how Thanksgiving went with the boyfriend."

"How different?" Gloria asked.

"Completely different," Nathan replied. "The only other people at the home on Thanksgiving were the butler, cook, and a maid. Tonight, we need to go to Foxborough to interview them simultaneously at their homes."

"Do you think they'll talk to us?" Hank asked.

"If they don't, we can always bring them in for questioning. We want to talk to them at the same time, so they can't call and warn each other."

"Or, coordinate their stories." Mac finished Nathan's sentence.

"There are three people to interview, but four of us. What's the fourth person going to do?" Gloria asked.

"I'm glad you asked that, Gloria. Since Mac isn't a police officer, I want you to accompany her to make it an official interview." Nathan stood to give each one of them a folder. "The name and address of the person you'll be visiting is at the top of the first page. I'll interview Patrick Spencer, the butler. Hank, you'll talk to the cook, Rose Oakley, and Gloria, you and Mac will speak with the maid, Barbara Sullivan. You'll find the rest of the file are the questions we need to know. Do your best to not ask leading questions. Lastly, if the person agrees to it, I'd like for you to record the interview with these." He gave them each a digital audio recorder. "Any questions?"

With no questions, Nathan added one more thing. "Don't worry about coming back here tonight. However, I'd like for you to meet here at eight in the morning."

Hank and Gloria left the office with their assignments, but Mac stopped Nathan he walked out. "Here's the list of people that signed the book at Ann's funeral." She handed him copies of several sheets of handwritten signatures.

He looked at the pages. "How did you get these so fast?"

"I had an associate visit the Parkers' last night to copy the sign-in book. They told them it was to help with the investigation, which it is."

"Thanks." Nathan put the pages into a folder, and headed out of the office.

****

Gloria sat in the police car in the rear parking lot, when Mac stepped out of the building and got into the car. Gloria had already programmed their destination into the car's GPS. They followed Nathan and Hank out of the parking lot, as the procession headed to Foxborough.

"This should be an interesting night," Gloria said, making small talk. It was going to be long drive, one that Gloria wasn't sure she was going to enjoy with Mac.

"I hope it proves productive," Mac said. "Especially since this was my idea."

"I think it was a good one. You were a police officer before becoming a private investigator, right?"

"Yes, eight years with the Boston PD, two in the homicide division. What about you? How long have you been with the department?"

"I've been here for five years. Unfortunately, all of them have been at the front desk."

"All of them? But, you're in the field now."

"It's only been since Nathan was hired that I've had the opportunity to occasionally do real police work."

"How so?" Mac asked.

"Chief Cabot never thought female officers should work

on the street."

"But I've seen females on patrol in town. He must have changed his opinion on that."

Gloria laughed. "He started coming around after I helped on a few cases, but more so after the new female mayor took office. Everything changed then."

"Why are you still at the front desk? You must have seniority over some of the other officers."

"That's my decision. I like helping Nathan with his investigations. Always being in the building means I'm readily available to him."

"I think there's more to it than that. Am I right?"

Gloria hesitated, unsure if she wanted to admit the main reason she didn't want to patrol. "Oh, what the hell. I want to keep working close to Nathan because I want to be Mystic's first female detective." She held her breath, sure Mac was going to laugh.

"I haven't been around you much, but I can recognize intelligence, confidence, and desire. You will make a very good detective someday, but in order to do that, you're going to need more field experience. You should reconsider transferring to the Patrol Division."

Gloria was sure if the sun was still up, Mac would see how flushed her face must have become. "Thank you. Please don't tell anyone about wanting to be a detective, especially Nathan."

"Don't worry, your secret is safe. When the time comes for you to interview for the position, you call me and we'll meet for lunch. I'll help you prepare."

"That would be nice."

Forty-five minutes later, they were in Barbara Sullivan's living room. The Parkers' maid sat on the couch, along with Gloria. She looked to be about thirty years old, and a slightly petite woman. Mac took a seat on a nearby chair.

"Miss Sullivan, I want to thank you for allowing us into your home," Gloria said. "As I said at the door, we'd like to talk to you about Ann Parker."

"Of course. I want to do what I can, but I don't think I know anything," Sullivan said.

"Before we go any further, do you mind if I record our conversation?" Gloria took the digital recorder out of her purse, placing it on the coffee table in front of them.

"I guess that will be okay," she answered.

"Good." Gloria pushed the record button. "This is Officer Gloria Wheeler interviewing Barbara Sullivan at her home. Also present is Private Investigator Mackenzie Dupont, assisting in the Ann Parker case. Miss Sullivan, are you employed by William and Margaret Parker as a housekeeper?"

"Yes, ma'am."

"Were you working at the Parkers' home on Thanksgiving of last year?

"Ah - yes."

"Was Ann Parker there with David Anders that day?"

"Yes, Miss Ann was there with Mr. Anders."

"Can you tell me what happened that day between Ann, her father, and Mr. Anders?" Gloria asked.

"I really don't feel right talking about this. I'm sure Mr. Parker wouldn't like it." Sullivan shifted around on the couch, obviously nervous. Her eyes darted from left to right, failing to make direct contact with Gloria or Mac.

"You want Ann's killer to be caught, right?"

"Of course." Now, she looked at Gloria. "But I don't know anything."

"This is just part of the information process. You may know more than you think."

"I understand." She cleared her throat. "Mr. Parker and Miss Ann argued about Mr. Anders. Mr. Parker didn't like him at all."

"Did Mr. Anders take part in the discussion?" Mac jumped in, asking.

"He tried, but Miss Ann kept telling him to be quiet."

"Are those the words she used, 'be quiet?'"

"No," Miss Sullivan lowered her head. "She told him to shut up. She actually had to tell him several times, until Mr. Anders stormed out."

"What happened after that?" Gloria asked.

Sullivan looked back up. "Miss Ann wasn't happy. Her uncle, Father Mike, tried to smooth things out between her and Mr. Parker, but she just got mad at him too."

"What was said between them?" Mac asked.

"He tried to bring them together through religion, quoting some Bible verses, but she wouldn't have it."

"Did she leave?" Gloria asked.

"No. Patrick went out to tell everyone that dinner was ready to be served. Everyone went into the dining room to eat. It was a very quiet meal."

"Did they talk at all?"

"Mrs. Parker tried to get a conversation going, but mostly there were only one or two-word replies to her questions."

"What about Mr. Anders? Did anyone get him to come back in for dinner?" Mac asked.

"No. It was like they completely forgot about him."

"Miss Sullivan, you have a very precise recollection of what happened that day," Mac said. "I thought you would have been working in the kitchen. How did you hear all of that?"

Sullivan's face became flushed, no doubt from embarrassment. "We all could hear the shouting from in the kitchen. They were so loud."

"I'm sure it didn't hurt that you all were probably lined up with your ears to the door," Mac said.

Gloria didn't like the direction Mac was taking the interview. "Miss Sullivan, is there anything else that happened that day you can think of?"

"I don't think so," she replied.

"What about Ann's relationship with her parents, after what happened on Thanksgiving?" Gloria asked.

"It was strained. Miss Ann didn't speak to her father

much after that, except when they argued about money, and her getting a job."

"She didn't want to work?"

"She told him she did, just not for his company."

"Mr. Parker wanted her to work for him?"

"Yes, as a vice-president of some department."

"Did she say why she didn't want the job?" Gloria asked.

"I don't remember."

Gloria looked over at Mac, who shrugged her shoulders. "I think we have everything we need. Thank you again for speaking with us." She handed her one of her cards. "If you think of anything else, don't hesitate to call me."

"I will." Miss Sullivan stood.

Gloria turned off the recorder and placed it back into her bag. She and Mac left the home for the drive back to Mystic.

****

The next morning, with coffee in hand, they all assembled in Nathan's office. "I stopped by the bakery to get doughnuts for us. Help yourself," Nathan said when they came in. He opened the box on his desk. Each of them took one. Once everyone had their food, Nathan was ready to begin. "I interviewed the butler last night, if you can call it that. He's very loyal to the Parkers."

"He didn't answer any questions?" Mac asked.

"Only a few. He mostly kept saying what Mr. Parker told me at my last visit is exactly what happened on Thanksgiving."

"He was in the room when you were last there?" Hank asked.

"No, but I'm sure he was within earshot."

"So, not much help," Gloria said.

"No, not much. Hank, how did you do with the cook, Mrs. Oakley?"

"Only a little better. Obviously, Mrs. Oakley didn't hear what Mr. Parker told you on Wednesday. She said Parker and

Ann had a huge argument about Anders, while he just sat there, not saying a word."

"He didn't say anything?" Gloria asked.

"Not a thing, according to the cook."

"What did the maid say, Gloria?" Nathan asked.

Gloria and Mac took turns explaining everything they learned from Barbara Sullivan.

Nathan let out an exasperating breath. "Well, we don't know much more than we did before, and we still can't rule Anders out as a suspect. Before I left Foxborough last night, I dropped by Anders apartment to speak to his roommates. They said the night of Ann's murder, Anders' car was parked in front of their apartment building when they got home from their night out."

"What time was that?" Mac asked.

"They thought around one-thirty a.m."

"Doesn't that rule him out?" Gloria asked.

"I'm afraid not. The roommates said when they got home, they were pretty wasted, but they remembered his bedroom door was closed. Since they all had to work the next morning, they went straight to sleep. When they got up the next morning for work, the door was still closed. They never saw him, so no alibi." Nathan's email dinged. He checked it. "Mallory sent the list of places Ann Parker met her other boyfriend here in Mystic. Hank, can you check out the places they met during the day?"

"I can do that this afternoon," Hank replied.

"Would you like me to help with the places they met at night?" Gloria asked.

"No. I'll take care of the rest of them." Nathan looked at Mac, who was sitting behind Gloria, shaking her head "no."

"Ah, on second thought, maybe you could take half of my list, Gloria." He looked again at Mac, who now nodded in agreement. "I'll divide the list up and send it to your phones, along with a photo of Ann for you to show at the restaurants. Thanks for helping with the interviews last night. Could you take your recorders to Mallory to upload the interviews and ask her to email them to me?"

Hank and Gloria left the office, but Mac stayed behind.

"What was with the head shaking? Nathan asked her.

"You were holding Gloria back. When you listen to the recording of her interview, you'll see that she did a fantastic job last night."

"I have never held Gloria back, but she has a job at the front desk to do."

"You sound like Chief Cabot now." Mac stood.

"If I pull her off the front desk, then someone else has to stop what they're doing to fill in. At that point, it's like a snowball rolling downhill."

"She could do it after hours, like last night."

The department does not like paying overtime," he pointed out. "You should have seen me begging to get OT pay for them last night."

"They need to get over that."

"We don't have the budget that the Boston PD does."

"If this department wants to get a detective division, they better get a better budget." She left the office.

"What the hell was that about?" Nathan asked himself out loud. Deciding not to dwell on it, he divided up the list of locations from Mallory, attached the photo of Ann, and emailed them to Hank and Gloria.

Right before lunch, Mallory appeared at Nathan's door. "Busy?"

"Not too busy. Come in."

She stepped in and sat down. She looked like she was about to burst. "I did it, or at least I think I did it."

"Did what?" he asked.

"I think I broke the code in Elizabeth Howe's date book."

"That's fantastic. What did you discover?"

She handed Nathan copies of some of the pages from the planner. "Almost every month, there are two days with the letters 'CM' listed. I went to the town library, and with the help of Mrs. Olsen, the librarian, I discovered that covens meet to celebrate eight Sabbats and thirteen Esbats. Those are the Wiccan holidays and celebrations. Those dates correspond to the CM's, coven meetings, in the date book."

He looked at the pages Mallory had given him. "You may just be right."

"There's a CM written on today's date," she pointed out.

"Any idea where the meeting will be held?"

"I looked through everything we found at both Miss Howe and Miss Parker's residences. I couldn't find anything that indicated a location of the meetings."

"I know someone who might know." Nathan stood, grabbed his jacket, and started out the door. "Great job, Mallory."

When he walked into the Magick Potions & Gifts store, he found it very busy, and what appeared to be two new employees. "Is Isabella here?" he asked one of them.

"She's doing a tarot reading for someone right now."

Nathan pulled one side of his jacket aside, showing the badge on his belt. "I need to speak with her as soon as possible."

"Yes, sir."

While he waited for Isabella, he browsed around the store. Because of the investigation, he had become intrigued with the practice of Wicca, and found himself in the part of the store where figurines were displayed. He remembered Dana's outburst the other day after he failed to return her call. *Maybe I should buy her something to help smooth things over*, he thought.

That's when he noticed two small figurines near the back of one shelf. They had no features, looking like two ghosts hugging each other; one orange, one white. Those would be perfect, he thought, and picked them up.

"Detective, you wanted to see me?"

He turned to find Isabella standing behind him. Dressed in her usual long black dress, pale skin makeup, and dark eyes.

"Yes. Is there somewhere we can talk in private?"

"We can go to my office." She led him to the back of the store. "Did you find something you liked?" she asked, referring to the hugging dolls.

"Yes. I have a friend who I think might like these. I'll pay for them before I leave."

Isabella opened the door to her office. They both stepped inside and sat down. "Those hugging dolls are my favorite thing in the store. I have a set myself." She motioned toward the shelf of items to the right of her desk. The exact set of hugging dolls were on it.

"I made a good choice then."

"What did you need to see me about?" she asked.

"We found something in Elizabeth Howe's date book that I think you might be able to help me with."

"I'll do what I can."

He handed her copies of the date book. "On the first Friday of each month, she has written CM, which we think means coven meeting. Are we right?"

She looked at each page before answering. "Yes, that's what it means."

Nathan was surprised that she answered, since she'd refused to help during his past visits. "Why the sudden decision to cooperate?"

"Because two members of my coven have been killed. I don't want it to happen to anyone else."

"You made the right decision. According to her book, there's a meeting tonight."

"That's correct."

"Can I attend?"

"No."

So much for cooperation, he thought. "Why not?"

"You wouldn't be welcomed by the others. We don't allow visitors to the ritual. Outsiders would not understand our magick. That's why we don't invite them."

"Will you at least ask them if I can meet with them

individually?"

"I'll ask, but I wouldn't count on any of them agreeing to it," she said.

"Do you think any of them might be involved in the murders?"

"Not if they're true Wiccans. For the coven to survive, there must always be love and harmony within the group."

"What if there's a problem between two members?"

"They are to work it out themselves, or one of them will be asked to leave."

"Did you know Ann Parker was in your group to gather information for a series of articles she was writing for a controversial newspaper in Boston?" he asked.

"I don't believe that."

"It's true."

"So, she wasn't a true Wiccan." Isabella looked shocked.

"I honestly don't know what she believed in." He stood. "Thanks for talking to me today."

"I can gift-wrap those dolls, if you want," she said.

"That would be great."

Isabella took the dolls to the counter to ring up the sale, and wrap them. She swiped Nathan's credit card, and handed it back to him with the receipt. She took a few steps down the counter to wrap them in a box.

"Is this for your girlfriend?" Isabella asked.

"Not exactly. It's a long story. It's for a special friend, and I think she'll like them."

Isabella laughed. "Ah, you're in the doghouse."

Nathan laughed too. "How did you know that? Is it a Wiccan thing?"

"No. It's from years of working in retail." She finished wrapping the gift, and handed it to him. "I hope it helps."

"Me too." He left the store. Once he was in the car, he decided to call Dana before driving back to work.

"Dana Tyler," she answered.

"It's Nathan."

"Goodbye."

"Wait, don't hang up."

"What do you want? I'm a little busy," she said.

"I called to apologize. I'm sorry I didn't return your call. I didn't realize how important it was."

"I appreciate your apology."

"Would you like to have dinner with me tonight?" he asked.

She waited a few seconds before answering. "I'd love to, but originally I was going to ask you to dinner at my place."

"I'd hate to invite myself to dinner at your place." He laughed. "How about this? We meet at Capt's for drinks after work. We can order take-out from there. Then, go to your place to eat it. My treat," he suggested.

"It's a date," she replied.

Chapter Eight

It's a rare occurrence for there to be two full moons in a month, but the first one was happening on this night. As High Priestess, Isabella was in charge of setting up the altar, which she had her dedicant do under her supervision. Allison, the dedicant, arrived at the field a few minutes after Isabella.

"As soon as you get the things out of my car, you may begin setting up the altar," Isabella said.

After unloading several boxes, Allison first covered the table with a black cloth, adding five candles, a pentagram, incense censer, a chalice, and finally an athame, a large, double-edged knife.

More people began arriving, including the High Priest, Joe Cassidy. "Good evening, Isabella."

"Good evening, Joe. I need to speak with you in private." They stepped away from the others.

"What is it?"

"Detective Perry came to see me today. He wants to talk to our members about Ann and Elizabeth."

"The identity of the coven members must remain sacred," he said.

"He wants me to ask them for permission to release their names to him. I was thinking maybe he should talk to them. If it helps find the killers, it would be worth it."

"No. I'll talk to him. We've known each other since high

school, he'll listen to me." Joe turned and walked back to the others, to help set out the cakes and wine.

Soon, it was time to begin the ritual. Isabella nodded for them to light the candles. "Members, please cast the circle," she announced.

The nine remaining members, along with the High Priest, formed a circle around the altar. Each member, both male and female, were dressed in black robes. On the north side of the circle was a stack of wood in a pit waiting to be lit.

"High Priest, please light the sacred fire," Isabella said.

Joe lit a propane torch, lowering it to the kindling. The fire lit immediately, thanks to a little accelerant he had sprayed on the wood earlier. Once it started burning well, he added the larger pieces to keep it going, then joined the others back in the circle.

Isabella began. "Before we pay homage to the Lord and Lady, I want to remind everyone that we have lost two members recently to horrific acts by someone. Because the two murdered were members of our coven, I feel we may also be targets. Please watch yourselves, and make sure you keep your amulets on your person for protection until this demon can be found. So mote it be."

"So mote it be," they all repeated.

Isabella continued paying homage to the Lord and Lady.
"Lord and Lady hear my plea,
Please rid this space of negativity,
Fill us all with your cleansing light,
And guide us through the sacred rites."

Each member in the circle took turns giving thanks until they reached the last member. Claire, the youngest member of the coven, bowed her head, then looked up to the stars. "I want to honor the lives of our sisters, Ann Parker and Elizabeth

Howe. May your persecutor be found and punished in a way equal to your fate. So mote it be."

"So mote it be," the group repeated.

"High Priest, please bid farewell to the Lord and Lady," Isabella requested.

The whole group turned to face north. Joe pick up the athame, holding it high, and recited.

"Merry do we meet,
Merry do we part, and
Merry till we meet again.
So mote it be."

"So mote it be." Isabella threw some powder on the fire, causing it to flare, then die back down. Everyone exchanged hugs and kisses, and the ritual was over.

"Please partake in the cakes and wine before you leave, should you desire." She waved her hand toward the table holding the refreshments. The group moved to the table.

While everyone enjoyed the food and casual conversation, Isabella started taking down the altar.

"Need any help?" Joe asked.

"Sure. Thanks."

Joe put the last of the items into a box. "I'll carry this one for you."

She carried one box, and Joe the other. They walked to her car, putting everything in the truck of Isabella's car. "Thanks for your help, Joe."

"Are you taking this stuff to your store?"

"Yes."

"I'd be glad to follow you there to help unload," he offered.

"I appreciate the offer, but it's just a couple boxes, and I park right next to the back door. I can handle it."

"If you're sure."

"I am. Please let me know what Detective Perry says

when you talk to him. I'm really worried about our members."

"Don't worry. Between their amulets and the Lord and Lady watching over them, I think they'll be fine," he said.

"I hope." She got into her car, and drove away.

****

Nathan spotted Dana as soon as he entered Capt's Waterfront Bar and Grill. She waited in a booth by the window looking out over the harbor. "Good evening," he said, bending down to kiss her on the cheek, then sitting across the table from her.

The waitress had followed Nathan to the table. "Can I get you something to drink?"

He saw Dana was having wine. "I'll have a whiskey sour, straight up." They also ordered their takeout food at the same time.

"Whiskey sour. Bad day today?" Dana asked.

"It was long, and I'm glad it's over. I bought you something today." He placed the gift-wrapped box on the table.

"Oh, my. What's the occasion?" She was grinning from ear to ear.

"No real occasion. I was a little absentminded the other day, and wanted to apologize. Open it."

Dana tore off the paper and opened the box. "Hugging dolls. They're beautiful." She put them on the table, pushing them together in a hug. "I love them. Thank you." She reached over, giving his hand a squeeze.

"I thought they looked like hugging ghosts, especially since I got them at the Magick Potions and Gifts shop."

"I don't care where you got them. I love them."

The waitress walked by, setting Nathan's drink on the table.

"Are you and the new girl getting along better?" He took a sip of his drink.

"More or less. She's good, and going to be at the paper

for a long time, so I need to get along with her, even if I don't like it. What's the saying? 'Keep your friends close, and your enemies closer.'"

"That's a good way to look at it."

"Any progress on the murder case?" she asked.

"Off the record?"

Dana smiled. "Off the record."

"We've had some progress, but not much."

"Any suspects?"

"A few, and that's on the record. You can also print that we believe both victims were practicing witches." He took another drink.

"You think witches are being targeted?"

"It's a possibility. Anyone in Mystic that practices witchcraft should be very careful."

"Can I quote you on that?"

"You can."

The waitress approached again. "Your take-out order is ready. Scott has it at the bar. You can pay there too."

"Thanks." Nathan took one last drink before he and Dana walked to the bar. Nathan paid the bill, and carried the bag holding their dinner outside to Dana's car. "I'll follow you to your house."

****

The full moon had long set when Nathan awoke the next morning. He rolled over to look at the other side of the bed. Then, he remembered he came home, alone, last night. Apparently, Dana wasn't as appreciative of his gift as he hoped she'd be, but that was okay. That wasn't really why he got it for her.

His cell phone started ringing. "Perry.... No, I was awake. What's up?.... What! How bad?.... I'll meet you there." He quickly got dressed, and rushed out the door.

It didn't take long for him to arrive at the hospital. He

hurried through the front entrance, immediately heading to the Intensive Care Unit. When he stepped off the elevator, he spotted Hank standing near the nurse's station.

"I hated calling you so early, but I thought it was urgent enough," Hank said.

"Tell me what happened."

"I worked the night shift last night, filling in for Officer Walker. I was about to go off-duty at six this morning when the call came in. Another female body found near the cemetery where Ann Parker was found. This time nearer to the road, and fortunately, the woman's still alive."

"She can't be in good condition, if she's in ICU," Nathan said.

"Come on, I'll take you back." Hank said something to one of the nurses at the station, and the double doors to ICU opened. Two rooms down the hall, Hank stopped by the glass door.

Nathan looked in. If he didn't know who she was, he'd never have recognized Isabella Osborne laying in the bed.

"What happened to her?"

"She was beaten, then pressed between two boards with heaving rocks on top," Hank replied. "She nearly suffocated from the weight of the rocks."

"Sexual assault?"

"The doctor said no."

"Who found her?"

"The cemetery crew was going out to dig a grave for a funeral. Whoever did this used the crew's backhoe to put the rocks on her."

"Where did the rocks come from?" Nathan asked.

"They find rocks when they dig a grave out there. They move them to the edge of the cemetery for later removal. These hadn't been removed yet."

Nathan continued to stare at Isabella. "Fingerprints on the backhoe?"

"I called Mallory right after I called you, and told the

gravediggers not to touch the machinery."

Nathan saw an African-American man with long, braided hair sitting in the corner of the room. He had a worried look on his face. "Who's the man?"

"That's her husband, Darius Johnson."

"Has she been conscious at all?"

"In and out, but not enough for questioning."

"I need to talk to her husband," Nathan said.

Hank tapped on the glass, and motioned for Darius to join them.

He came out of the room.

"Darius, this is Detective Perry. He has some questions for you," Hank said.

"Sure."

They stepped away from the door, but still within sight of Isabella. "Mr. Johnson, do you know anyone who would want to hurt your wife?" Nathan asked.

He looked back at his wife. "No. Everyone loves Isabella."

"I know there was a coven meeting last night. Was she there?"

Darius looked back at Nathan. "Those meetings are usually secret. How did you know?"

"I talked to Isabella yesterday about the two members of the group that were murdered."

Darius' eyes widened. "You think her attack was related to the murders?"

"It's possible. Where were you last night?"

"Me? You think I did this to my wife?" He was getting a little loud.

"It's just a routine question we always ask the spouse," Hank explained.

"I'm an assistant manager at a warehouse down at the harbor. I got called in about eight p.m. for an emergency. I didn't get home until sunrise this morning. You can ask my manager. He was there with me all night."

Hank looked at Nathan. "I'll take care of that, so we can

clear him."

"Back during the Witch Trials, they killed witches by pressing them under boulders. That's what someone was trying to do to her, right?" Darius' voice cracked as he spoke.

"Are you Wiccan also?" Nathan asked.

"I am, but I belong to a different coven."

"Why a different one?"

Darius watched a nurse go into Isabella's room. "I belong to a different group because of her status."

"What does that mean?" Nathan asked.

"She's the High Priestess of her coven," Darius said.

The nurse walked out of the room, retrieved the doctor, and both went back in. Darius followed them, and the nurse closed the curtain.

"Did you see what was going on?" Nathan asked Hank.

"No."

The nurse came out of the room.

"What's going on?" Nathan asked.

"She's waking up." The nurse continued past them, getting some medication out of a cabinet, then returning to the room.

The officers waited to see how Isabella was. Several minutes later, Darius came out from the room. "They think she's going to be okay."

"That's good to hear," Hank said.

"How is she feeling?" Nathan asked.

"She's still pretty groggy, but said she hurt from head to toe, especially when she takes a breath."

"That's understandable. We really need to talk to her about what happened. When do you think she'll feel like it?"

"I don't know. I guess, it'll be up to the doctor. You should probably check back tomorrow," Darius said.

The nurse stuck her head out. "Mr. Johnson, she's asking for you."

Darius stepped back into the room with the nurse.

"We need to have her blood checked for Valium," Nathan

told Hank.

"Why?"

"Both Ann Parker and Elizabeth Howe had Valium in their system."

"I'll have the nurse tell the doctor we need that information." They stopped by the nurse's station to make that request. On their way out through the double-doors, they nearly knocked someone down.

"Hey, watch where you're going," the man said. "Oh, Nathan, it's you."

Nathan looked at the man, surprised by who it was. "What are you doing here, Joe?"

"I'm here to check on Isabella Osborne."

"How do you know Isabella?"

"Oh. Well, I, ah, I guess I shouldn't have said that."

"Let's go sit down and talk, Joe." Nathan took him by the arm, leading him to a nearby waiting area. The three men sat down. "Well, let's hear it?"

"This is going to really come as a surprise to you. There's something about me that very few people know," Joe said.

Puzzled, Nathan waited for him to continue.

Joe leaned toward them. "I'm a Wiccan, and a member of Isabella's coven. To be more precise, I'm the High Priest of the coven," he said, in almost a whisper.

Nathan was speechless. How could simple-minded Joe Cassidy become a High Priest? Had he underestimated him? "Why didn't you tell me this at the police station the other day?"

"Most of us like to keep our spirituality private," he replied.

"You were at the meeting last night?" Nathan asked.

"Yes."

"What happened to Isabella?" Hank asked.

"I don't know. She left after the meeting. I stayed to partake in cakes and wine with the others," he answered.

Nathan wasn't sure if he believed him, or not.

"The ritual, that's what we call the meeting, started at eight, as the full moon rose. We finished around nine, and she left not long afterward."

"She didn't stay for the refreshments?" Hank asked.

"Cakes are not refreshments," Joe said very matter-of-factly. "Cakes are a ceremonial snack that the coven shares after the ritual is over, by giving thanks to the Goddess."

"Who's the Goddess?" Nathan asked.

Joe looked at Nathan as if he'd been insulted. "The Goddess is the female essence of All. She is in everything, and is everything." He paused. "I have to go." He quickly walked away.

"What the hell? Want me to stop him?" Hank asked.

"No, but Joe is definitely not working on this investigation."

By Monday morning, Isabella had been moved to a regular room, and was sitting up in bed, having just finished her breakfast, when Nathan stepped into her room. Aside from the bruises, she looked different than she did at her at her store. Her normally spiked hair was now flat against her scalp, with bangs hanging over her forehead. He was surprised to see that without her goth-like makeup, she had a very pleasing, and healthy-looking, complexion.

"Good morning, Detective." She sat her hot tea on the tray in front of her.

"Good morning. You certainly look better than you did when I saw you Saturday morning, and different than I'm used to seeing you."

She chuckled. "You're seeing the real me now."

"I like this look. How are you feeling?" he asked.

"Much better, even though I've been poked, prodded, and x-rayed. Fortunately, I have no broken bones, and they took me off the oxygen last night. I'm still sore and bruised, but I feel better."

"I'm glad to hear it. I guess you know that I'm here officially. I need to ask you some questions."

"Sure. Go ahead."

Nathan pulled a chair over to her bed. He sat down, pulling out his notepad and pen from his jacket pocket. "What time did you leave your meeting Friday night?"

"The ritual started at eight, and lasts about an hour. I packed away the items from the altar, and probably left around nine-thirty."

"Joe Cassidy told me he was at the meeting. He even said something about being the High Priest. Is that true?"

"He told you that?" she asked.

"He did. He came to the hospital Saturday morning to check on you." Nathan thought he saw Isabella shiver when he said that. "Are you okay?"

"Joe is the High Priest, a creepy High Priest."

Nathan now understood her reaction.

"He helped me load the boxes into my car, then offered to follow me to my shop where I store everything until the next meeting. I told him no."

"How did he react to that?"

"I'm not sure. We only had the light of the full moon, and it was setting, so I really couldn't see his face that well. He tried to insist, but I told him I didn't need any help."

"Tell me what happened after you left the meeting."

"I drove to my shop."

"Did you notice any cars following you?" he asked.

"I didn't notice. It was a Friday night in October, so there was a lot of traffic in town."

Nathan shook his head in agreement. "When you got to the store, where did you park?"

"I always park in the ally behind the store, next to the back door."

Nathan made some notes as she recounted the night. "Did you unload the car?"

"Yes. I put the boxes just inside the door, to put away the next day. I locked up, walked back to my car, and that's all I remember."

"Is that your same routine after every meeting?"

"Yes, I suppose it is. I hadn't thought of that," she said.

"I'll have someone check to see if your car is still there." He jotted that in his notebook. "How long does it take you to get to the store from the meeting location?"

"Maybe thirty minutes with the traffic."

He wrote more notes. "Did you hear anything before you blacked out?"

"I don't remember hearing anything."

"Do you think Joe may have left to follow you, after you left the meeting?"

"When I drove away after the ritual had concluded, I saw Joe walking back to the group for cakes and wine. He was responsible for the cleanup."

"I'm going to need to talk to someone from your group to verify how long Joe stayed after there."

Isabella didn't say anything.

"We have to find out who did this," he said.

"You can talk to Joy Burns."

"Joy Burns." He wrote her name down.

"Darius can give you her number."

"Did someone say my name?" Darius walked into the room, and gave his wife a kiss.

A nurse followed him in, carrying a bag. "Detective, these are Miss Osborne's clothes and the personal items she was wearing when admitted. They've been locked up in the ER until we knew you were back." She put the bag on a chair, then handed him an envelope. "This is the toxicology screen you asked for."

Nathan took the envelope. "Thank you."

The nurse left.

"Can I have my stuff?" Isabella asked.

"I'm sorry, no, not yet. We need to go over everything for evidence first. Once the crime lab is finished with it, I'll see to it that you get it all back. There is one thing, though. I do need for you to look through everything to see if any of your personal effects are missing." He pulled a pair of latex gloves from a box on the wall for her to wear. She gave him a puzzled look. "You don't want to get any blood on you that might remain." He handed her the bag.

She put the gloves on and opened the bag.

"Don't take anything out of the bag, just let me know if anything is missing," he said.

"Okay. Oh, Darius, Detective Perry needs Joy's phone number so he can find out what time Joe Cassidy left the ritual that night."

"Joe Cassidy? Why do you need to know when he left?" Darius asked.

Nathan looked at Isabella.

"You think he did this, don't you?" Darius asked. "'Cause if he did, I'll kill that motherfucker."

"Darius!" Isabella shouted.

"You said he was always creeping you out. I don't know why you never removed him from the coven."

"He's the High Priest. You know it would be practically impossible for me to do that."

"You're the High Priestess. You could do it."

Nathan needed to take control of his conversation. "Regardless, Mr. Johnson, please stay away from Joe. I don't want to have to arrest you for murder. Isabella, have you finished looking through the bag?"

Darius took his phone out and started scrolling through it.

"It's not here!" Isabella frantically started looking through the bag.

"What's missing?" Nathan asked.

"My amulet. My amulet is missing." She was nearly in tears.

Darius walked over and held her. "Izzy, I'm sorry."

"This amulet, was it valuable?" Nathan asked.

"Yes," she replied. She sat back in bed. "It's a sapphire, but the value isn't important."

"A sapphire amulet is worn for its protective power," Darius explained.

"We'll look behind your shop for it, and where they found you Friday night. Darius, do you have a photo of it?"

"Yes, I do." He looked through the photos on his phone, finally showing Nathan a picture of Isabella wearing the sapphire.

"That's beautiful. Can you send it to my phone?" Nathan handed one of his cards to Darius. He turned to Isabella. "Would Ann and Elizabeth also have worn a sapphire amulet?"

"I don't know about Elizabeth. I hadn't got to know her very well. Ann wore a Ruby amulet," she said.

Nathan made more notes in his book. "Thank you for talking with me today. I'll let you know if we come up with anything." He picked up the bag and started to leave.

"Wait," Isabella said. "Did you find Ann and Elizabeth's Book of Shadows?"

"Book of what?"

"Book of Shadows," she repeated. "Every witch keeps one. It's like a magical diary. It contains information about rituals, spells, and potions."

"Like a spell book? Yes, we found those at both of their homes."

"Can I have them?" she asked.

"We have them logged in as evidence. Why do you want them?"

"When a member of the coven dies, the High Priestess decides what happens to the member's book," Darius explained. "Usually, the coven will burn it during a ritual."

"I'd like to have a ceremony to burn them," Isabella said.

"Once I don't need them any longer, I'll see that you get them."

"Thank you."

"Here's the phone number you needed for Joy." Darius handed him a piece of paper.

Nathan took it and left.

Chapter Nine

With traffic being a nightmare, Nathan arrived at his office late the next morning. He was reading his email when Mac stuck her head in.

"Morning, Nathan," she greeted.

"Good morning. Where have you been? I don't think I've seen you for days."

She stepped into the office and sat down. "I went back to Boston to talk to Michael Aldridge."

Nathan's mind raced a mile a minute, trying to remember who that was.

"Seriously, you don't remember who that is?"

"Do you know how many different names I hear in a day?" he snapped back.

Mac just shook her head. "Michael Aldridge is the editor at the paper where Ann Parker worked. The one that kicked us out of his office because of you."

"Oh yeah, I remember now." He laughed. "What did Aldridge have to say?"

"He was much more forthcoming since you weren't there. He said Ann was getting some threatening mail about the research she was doing for the witchcraft articles."

"So, someone knew she was writing them."

"Apparently so." She pulled several pages of computer-printed letters out of her bag and placed them on his desk.

Nathan quickly browsed though them. "They are threatening, and they're not signed. Where are the envelopes?"

"Yeah---they didn't keep the envelopes," she said.

"Super. No chance of a DNA match, and the whole newspaper office probably handled the letters, so we'd probably only get fingerprint smudges."

"All right, all right, point taken, but they're still evidence of threats," she pointed out.

"You're right. I'll give them to Mallory to log in for Ann's case." He took an evidence bag out of his desk and put the letters inside. He filled out the information on the front of the bag, then both he and Mac signed it.

Gloria and Hank stepped into the office. "Good, you're both here," Gloria said.

"What's up? Nathan asked.

Gloria sat down, but Hank remained standing. She did her best to stay professional, but could barely contain herself. "I found Ann Parker's boyfriend."

"You did?" Nathan looked up at Hank, who nodded "yes." He continued, "That's great. Good job."

"How did you do it?" Mac asked.

"Saturday night, I went to the places on the list where he and Ann supposedly went on their dates, and at one of the places, I found someone who recognized the photo of Ann. They checked their past reservations and came up with a name. Brian Springer."

"That's excellent work," Nathan said. "Now, we need to find him."

"Well...I sort of already did."

"You already spoke to him?"

"No. I wouldn't do that without contacting you first." She handed Nathan a printout. "I found him on social media."

He looked at the paper. "He works at Judson's Jewelry Store here in Mystic. That explains his email address. Gloria, you've done it again. Call him to come in to talk to us."

"Will do." She got up to leave, but stopped. "Talk to us?"

"Yes, you and me. You found him. You should be in on the interview."

"Thank you." She started to leave.

"Wait, just a minute. I want to give an update while you're all here," Nathan said.

She sat back down.

"Hank already knows most of this, but the rest of you need to be caught up." He took a drink of his coffee. "We have another victim, but this one is still alive. Isabella Osborne was attacked after the coven meeting Friday night. She's in the hospital, but doing well."

"What happened to her?" Mac asked.

Nathan nodded to Hank to answer.

"Miss Osborne was found at the same cemetery as Ann Parker. The difference is that she was found between two boards with heavy rocks on top."

"She was pressed like they did to witches?" Gloria asked.

"Yes," Hank replied. "Nathan and I went to the hospital early Saturday morning. She was unconscious, so we couldn't talk to her. We did speak with her husband." He looked at Nathan. "I talked to the supervisor at his work this morning. He confirmed his alibi."

"That's good. We can take him off the suspect list," Nathan said. "Let me continue with what happened, when we were leaving Isabella's room. We ran into Joe Cassidy just outside of ICU."

"What was he doing there?" Mac asked.

"He was there to check on Isabella. She's the High Priestess of the coven and, get this, Joe is the High Priest."

"That little twerp who was in my office the other day is the High Priest?" Mac asked.

"Yes." Nathan tried to hide a snicker. "I went to see Isabella this morning at the hospital. She's doing well, and they moved her to a regular room. She'll probably be able to go home soon."

"That's wonderful," Gloria commented.

"She also told me that Joe is a little creepy around her at the meetings."

"No surprise there," Mac said.

"After the meeting on Friday night, she said he kept asking if she needed help unloading the boxes of stuff from her car into her store. She told him no."

"I don't blame her," Gloria said.

Nathan continued. "She was attacked in the ally behind her store. Other than that, she doesn't remember anything else. Hank, take Mallory down there to see if you two can find anything."

"I'm on it," Hank said, leaving the room.

"We need to add Joe to the suspect list," Nathan said.

"He definitely needs to be questioned," Mac said.

Nathan nodded his head in agreement. "Gloria, see if you can get Brian Springer in here tomorrow morning."

"I'll go contact him now." She left.

Mac looked at Nathan. "So, now what?"

"I think we need to go talk to Joe."

"You don't want him to come in here for questioning?"

"Not yet. This will be an unofficial visit, but we need to see how well he knew Ann Parker and Elizabeth Howe."

Nathan's phone buzzed. The display showed it was Gloria. He pushed the speaker button. "Yes."

"Dana Tyler is on line three for you," she said.

He looked at Mac.

"You better not ignore her this time."

Nathan agreed. "Thanks, Gloria. I'll talk to her." He pushed the button for line three. "Hello, Dana. You're on speaker, and Mac Dupont is in the room with me."

"Hello to both of you. I received the department's press release about the attack over the weekend. There wasn't much on the victim's condition, and the hospital won't release any information. Can you update me with anything?"

"I spoke with Miss Osborne this morning. She's out of

ICU, and doing better. She doesn't remember anything about the attack. Other than that, I don't have anything else," Nathan said.

"If she's in a regular room, is she able to have visitors?"

"That would be up to her doctor. My visit was an official one to question her about what happened."

"I see," Dana replied.

Nathan could tell she was taking notes of the conversation. "Just remember, her injuries were severe enough to be admitted to the ICU after a brutal attack. Give her a little time before talking to her."

"I understand that, but I do have a job to do. I'll let her decide if she wants to talk, but thank you again, for telling me how to do my job."

"Dana." Too late, she'd already hung up.

"You're in the doghouse again," Mac said.

"Doghouse? No, that's just her kidding around. We better go see Joe." *Yeah, I'm in the doghouse again*, he thought to himself.

****

Nathan opened the door to Joe Cassidy's office, letting Mac enter first. Today, an attractive young lady sat behind the front desk.

She looked at the clock on the wall, then at Nathan and Mac. "Good morning. How can I help you?"

"I need to see Joe," Nathan said, showing his badge.

"You don't have an appointment," she replied.

Nathan turned to look at the empty lobby, and then back at the receptionist. "Do I need one?"

"Mr. Cassidy likes to know ahead of time what his schedule is for the day."

"Could you tell Mr. Cassidy that Nathan Perry is here to see him."

She picked up the phone, and pushed two buttons.

"There's a Nathan Perry here to see you."

"The door to Joe's office opened practically before the girl put the receiver down. Joe nearly tripped over his own feet coming out. "Nathan, to what do I owe the pleasure of your visit?"

"Joe." Nathan nodded. "You remember Mac Dupont."

"I do, indeed. Please, come back to my office." Joe led them down the hallway. "Let's sit here." He motioned to a couch and chair, now in his office.

"This is new," Nathan said, sitting on the flowered couch. Mac also sat on the couch; Joe on the matching chair.

"I used the money I was reimbursed from helping you look for that rare coin in Boston to buy it. Do you like what I got?"

"They're nice, Joe."

"I thought so. I got them at an estate sale."

"We needed to talk to you about Isabella Osborne," Nathan said.

Joe's expression went somber. "Oh, it was a horrible thing to happen to her."

"It was brought to our attention that you've made some of the ladies at your coven meetings uncomfortable," Mac said.

"I don't understand. How have I made them uncomfortable?" He looked back and forth between Nathan and Mac.

"Apparently, you don't like taking no for an answer," Nathan said.

"I get it." Joe stood and started pacing. "I kept asking a couple ladies out for coffee, and when I wouldn't give up after they said no, they think I'm a stalker."

"If you recall, I nearly arrested you outside of a lady's home last year when you were taking pictures through a window."

He stopped pacing. "I told you that I was on a divorce case, and you let me go."

"But I never followed up on that to see if you really were on a case."

Joe remained standing with a scowl forming on his face.

"Did you ask Ann Parker or Elizabeth Howe to have coffee?" Mac asked.

"Yes, but---wait, you think I had something to do with their murders?"

"You know how this works. We have to talk to anyone with a connection to rule them out." Nathan hoped he'd convinced him that's why they were there.

"Oh. Okay. I understand," Joe replied. "What do you need to know?" Joe sat back down on the chair.

Nathan and Mac looked at each other with great success. Nathan began, "How well did you know Miss Parker and Miss Howe?"

"They were both members of the coven," Joe said.

"The coven you're the High Priest of?" Mac asked.

"Yes."

"I gotta ask, how did you become the High Priest?" Nathan asked.

"I've been a member of the coven for a long time, and I did a lot of studying."

"Do you really believe in this stuff?"

"Nathan, when I was a kid, my mother crammed her religion down my throat. It was church three nights a week and twice on Sunday. I finally stopped going when I got old enough that she couldn't make me go."

"That doesn't explain how you got into Wicca," Mac said.

"During my last year of high school, I had a crush on this girl who dressed in black all the time. She was weird, and had no friends, which worked to my advantage. I started sitting with her at lunch every day, and she introduced me to Wicca. She moved away before the end of the school year, but I had found my religion."

"Ann Parker was killed on the night of September twenty-third. Elizabeth Howe on the twenty-sixth. Do you know where you were on those nights?" Nathan asked.

"I was home."

"Alone?" Mac asked.

"Yes."

"You answered pretty fast, Joe. How do you know you were home on those nights? Don't you want to look at a calendar?" Nathan noticed beads of sweat forming on Joe's forehead.

"Maybe you both should leave." Joe stood. "If you want to talk to me again, I'll need to call a lawyer."

Nathan looked at Mac. "We better go." They left the office, walking out to the lobby, with Joe following. "Thanks, Joe."

Nathan stopped on the sidewalk.

"What's wrong? Aren't we going back to the department?" Mac asked.

"You are, I'm not. Would you mind walking back? It's not that far," Nathan said.

"Where are you going?"

"I've got an appointment with a banker. I need to go alone."

"Personal business?" she asked.

"My business." He walked to his car and drove off, leaving Mac standing on the sidewalk. He felt bad not telling her why he was going to the bank, but she worked for William Parker, and whether she liked it or not, he was a suspect in his daughter's murder. It was best she not be included in this part of the investigation.

Nathan now sat in the lobby of the Mystic State Bank, waiting to speak to Robert Clark, Vice-president.

"Detective Perry, if you'll follow me." Robert Clark, Bobby to his friends, was the typical banker, three-piece suit, clean-shaven, and every hair in place.

They stepped into his lavish office and both sat down. "Here's the warrant you needed. I want to make sure this is all official." He handed the document to Clark.

"Thank you." He looked it over. "This seems to be in order. Here is the account information you said you needed. It was a terrible thing that happened to Miss Parker." He handed Nathan a printout.

"Yes, it was." Nathan looked over the document.

"I'm curious. How did you figure out that Miss Parker's account was at this bank, rather than a larger one in Boston?"

"Her weekly paychecks from her employer were deposited here." Finished looking at the printout, Nathan put it into his portfolio. "Did her father, William Parker, ever contact you about her account?"

"No, but the bank in Foxborough that issued the certified check did."

"Do you remember when that was?"

"If you'll let me look at that printout again, I can narrow it down." Nathan handed the printout back to him. "The account was opened on January 10th with that check, and they called a couple days later," Clark said.

"Wouldn't releasing information that she had an account here violate privacy laws?" Nathan asked.

Clark adjusted his tie. "Normally, we wouldn't give out that information, but the bank said since the check was such a large one, they needed to confirm her address for their records."

"Is it common for a bank to do that?"

"We've never had that situation before, but each bank has their own policies."

"Is this the only account she had here?"

"Yes."

"It's a checking account. That's a lot of money to put into a checking account. Didn't anyone suggest that she might want to put the majority of it into a savings account, CD's, or invest it?"

"I was the one that opened her account, and yes, I did ask her about that. She said she preferred keeping it in the checking because she didn't know how long she'd be living in

Mystic," Clark said.

"A bank vice-president opened the account? Do you do that often?"

"I hadn't been promoted yet. I was still just a supervisor. The person that normally does that job was off that day, so I took over for her."

Nathan looked over his notes. "One last thing, has anyone else contacted the bank about Miss Parker or her account?"

"Not to my knowledge, but the calls don't normally come to me. If someone called to ask about an account that didn't belong to them, they would be told that any account information is confidential except to account owners. Even then, there's a series of questions the person has to answer to verify their identity before we release anything to them."

Nathan jotted down that information, and then stood. "Bobby, thank you very much for your cooperation." They shook hands.

"If there's anything else you need, let me know; with a warrant, of course." They both laughed.

Before going back to the police department, he stopped to pick up something for lunch. Now, at his desk, between bites of a hamburger and fries, he looked over the printout from the bank.

"Working lunch today?"

He looked up from his desk. "Most days. What brings the top state police detective to my humble office?"

Sam Denzinger stepped in and sat down. "I brought you something." He handed Nathan a file folder.

"What's this?" He looked through the thin file. "They found a woman in Salem that was burned at the stake?"

"Not just any woman, but a self-proclaimed, modern-day witch. They found her near where the convicted witches were burned in 1692. Someone called in the fire, and when the fire department got there, they found the body.

Nathan looked at the file again. "There's definitely

similarities with our murders, but not much detail in the report, not even an autopsy report."

"You know how long it takes to get an autopsy done, and they don't have the connection that you have with the top state police detective in order to put a rush on it," Denzinger joked.

"Do you think the top state police detective could put a rush on it now?"

"I did it this morning."

"While I'm thinking about it, the tox screen showed Valium in both of the ladies' blood," Nathan said.

"That's interesting. You think someone slipped it to them?"

"That's what I was thinking."

"I'll make sure the lab checks the Salem victim to see if it's possible to find any Valium in her system. I told the Salem PD that I would get them a copy of the files on your murders. Can I get those?"

"Sure. No problem."

"Thanks. I understand another witch was attacked here, but survived," Denzinger said.

"How'd you hear that?"

"I read it in the paper," Denzinger responded. "Any Valium in her system?"

"No. The hospital report showed none," Nathan said. "Isabella Osborne owns a witch shop in town. She was attacked behind her shop after leaving a coven meeting. The next morning, she was found at the cemetery where Ann Parker was found, and was pressed between two boards with heavy rocks on top. Fortunately, she was found before it was too late."

"Isabella Osborne? Didn't she report Ann Parker missing when I was here before?" Denzinger asked.

"Yes. She employed Ann at her store. She's also the High Priestess of the coven the two women belonged to." He picked up his phone, punching in three numbers. "Gloria, would you print two copies of Ann Parker, Elizabeth Howe, and Isabella Osborne's files for Detective Denzinger? Thanks." He replaced the receiver. "The second copy is for you."

"Thanks," Denzinger replied. "Your first victim was hanged, the second drowned, and the third pressed. Salem's victim was burned at the stake. We've got a real sick killer on our hands. Who are your suspects?"

"All of my suspects, but one, are connected only to Ann Parker; two former boyfriends, her father, and Joe Cassidy. So far, only Joe knew all three victims." Nathan sat back in his chair.

"Joe Cassidy? Isn't that the guy who fancies himself as a PI?"

"That's him, and technically he is a PI. The state issued him a license. He's also the High Priest of the coven," Nathan said.

"Him? My God. Do you think he's your killer?"

"He's a good candidate, but I'm not feeling it. I still have to question Ann Parker's last boyfriend. Until then, I'm leaning toward her father."

"Why the father?" Denzinger asked.

"Yes, why her father?" Mac stepped into the office.

Nathan hadn't noticed her at the door, and had hoped to wait a little longer before telling her about his theory. "I realize he's your employer, but I still can't get over the feeling that something wasn't right between them."

"You actually think he would kill his own daughter?"

"I'm not sure, but it wouldn't be the first time something like that happened between a father and daughter. I just want to add him to the suspect list."

"All because you have a feeling?" She folder her arms in front of her.

Nathan looked at Denzinger, who just smiled.

"Mr. Parker knew all along where his daughter was," Nathan said. "When she deposited her trust fund money, his bank was able to find out what bank she used. I think he got her contact information from them. It doesn't mean he killed her, but for whatever reason, he lied to us about not knowing where she was."

Mac, still in the doorway, stood speechless. Her shocked expression told Nathan that Parker may have kept this information from her also.

"Well, I think I had better get back to work," Denzinger said, breaking the uncomfortable silence. "I'll pick up those files from Gloria on my way out."

"Thanks for bringing Salem's file to me," Nathan said.

Denzinger nodded as he stood to leave.

Mac moved to her right, to let Denzinger out of the office. Now that they were alone, Mac sat in the chair just vacated by Denzinger. "That's the bank appointment you went to today, wasn't it?"

"Yes."

"Didn't you think you could trust me?" she asked.

"It's not that. You're connected to Parker. You know as well as I do, I couldn't take you with me. I planned on telling you as soon as I got back. I was going over Ann's bank records when Sam came in. Then, you showed up, and here we are." He handed her his notes and the printout from the bank visit.

She read over them. "He's known since January that she's been here? Why did he even hire me to try and find her, if he already knew?" she asked.

"Maybe to throw us off his scent."

"He'd have to know we'd eventually find out."

"We're a small department. He could have thought I'd miss it," Nathan said.

"He knew my reputation, and he hired me anyway." Obviously mad, she tossed the notes onto Nathan's desk.

"If he's involved, he probably thought he could outsmart us. Most criminals think that way, you know that. I'll have him come in for questioning. We'll get to the bottom of it."

"Damn right, we will." She let out a deep breath. "I know you're trying to make me feel better. Thanks. What was

Detective Denzinger here for?"

"He brought a case file to me from Salem. They found a woman burned at the stake last night. He told them about our murders and they were interested. He brought a copy of their file, and I'm sending them a copy of ours. Hopefully, between the two departments, one of us can figure something out." He handed her the folder from Salem.

She looked through it briefly. "It sure looks like it could be the same guy. What can I do to help?"

"Do you have any connections in Salem?"

"I know one or two people there I could talk to."

"Why don't you start there?"

Gloria interrupted them. "I'm sorry to intrude, but I just spoke to Brian Springer. He agreed to come in tomorrow morning to talk to us about Ann Parker. He sounded like a really nice young man."

"Thanks, Gloria. I hope he is," Nathan said. She left the doorway, walking toward the break room.

"I'm going to have Gloria question him with me, but can you be here to observe, read his body language, and anything else you might notice?"

"Yes. I'll be here." Mac stood. "I'm going to my office, to make some calls."

"I think I'm going to head out for the day. I've got plans for tonight."

"A date with your reporter?"

"My reporter?" he asked.

"Well, I didn't want to call her your girlfriend." Mac laughed, as she left the office.

"See you tomorrow." Before leaving, Nathan had one phone call he needed to make. After making that call, he got his coat from the hook on the wall, and put it on. He stopped by the break room. "Gloria, I'm leaving for the day. Call me on my cell, if you need me."

She looked up from her conversation at a table full of other officers. "Will do."

Witch Hunt

****

Ding-Dong.

Dana threw the towel into the hamper and tied her robe around her.

Ding-Dong.

She pulled the second towel from her head. There was no time to do anything with her wet hair, but run her fingers through it. She hurried from the bathroom, through the bedroom, and up the hallway.

Ding-Dong.

"I'm coming. I'm coming." She opened the door without first checking to see who it was. He rushed in and closed the door before she could stop him.

"You could catch a cold with that wet hair," he said.

"What are you doing here, Nathan?"

"I brought dinner." He held up two bags of food from The Witch's Brew.

She shook her head from side to side.

"If I would have called first, would you have let me come over?"

"No."

"And, that's why I just showed up, unannounced."

She tried to hold back a smile, but failed. "Take the food to the kitchen while I get dressed."

Nathan carried the food into the kitchen, as Dana turned toward the bedroom.

She now looked in the mirror. Her hair was going in all directions. *I can't believe I answered the door looking like this.* She picked up a brush and hair dryer, and started working on her hair.

Thirty minutes later, she was dressed in a sweater and jeans, and her hair was perfect. With just a light touch of makeup, she was ready for dinner. When she walked into the kitchen, she couldn't believe what she saw. Nathan had set the table for two, complete with wine and candles.

141

"Look what you did," she said. "What's the occasion?"

He held the chair for her as she sat down. "I'm still apologizing for being a jerk a few days ago." He joined her at the table, and began serving the food.

Chapter Ten

Officers were shuffling out of the roll call room as Nathan arrived to work. Hank and Gloria walked out into the hallway as he was unlocking his office door.

"Hank, isn't that Detective Perry just getting to work?" Gloria asked.

Nathan cringed upon hearing her comment. Since he was late, he had hoped to come in quietly this morning.

"Why yes, I believe it is," Hank added, laughing.

Nathan opened his door, just as Mac walked up. They all followed him into the office.

"Long night with the reporter?" Mac asked.

Nathan put his coffee on his desk, and then hung up his coat before sitting down.

"That's not your regular travel mug," Gloria said.

"My off-duty evenings are none of your concern," he said, partly joking, partly not. "Gloria, what time is Brian Springer supposed to be here?"

"He should be here around nine."

"Good. I want you with me, and Mac will watch from the observation room."

"Do you need me for anything?" Hank asked.

"Did you and Mallory find anything in the alley behind Isabella's store?"

"No. Her car was missing, and there were no security

cameras in the ally either. However, we did check with some nearby businesses and found a couple that have cameras facing the street. Mallory is waiting for the videos now."

"Hopefully, we'll see either Isabella's car or the suspect's car drive by," Nathan said.

"Mallory and I have been monitoring online auction sites to see if Isabella's amulet shows up," Gloria said. "We'll watch for Ann's ruby also."

"Hank, can you check with pawn shops and second-hand stores in Mystic for the necklaces?" Nathan asked.

Hank nodded.

The perpetrator may have kept them as a souvenir. Serial killers are known to do that," Mac said.

Nathan's intercom buzzed. "Yes."

"Detective, there's a Brian Springer here to see you."

"Thanks. I'll be with him in a few minutes."

"He's early," Gloria said.

"If you don't need me for anything, I should be getting on patrol and start checking those shops for the necklaces," Hank said.

"Thanks, Hank. I'll keep you updated. Gloria, would you bring Mr. Springer to Interrogation Room one?"

"Yes, sir. I'll go get him right now." She left.

"So, how was your date last night?" Mac asked.

"Please don't bring up my personal life at work." He started looking through his desk for a notebook.

"Sorry."

"I don't like sharing my personal time with my coworkers."

"You think they don't know you're sleeping with the reporter? Hell, I knew the first time I met her at the café."

"I know they know about us, but I don't want people thinking she and I are a couple, because we're not."

"Touchy subject," Mac said.

"Damn right, it is." He found his notebook, picked up the case file, and stood. "We need to go. Gloria is waiting."

They walked down the hallway, where Gloria was waiting

for them. "Is he ready?" Nathan asked.

"Yes. He's inside. He seems like a nice young man," Gloria said.

"You keep saying that. You know looks can be deceiving."

"I know." She looked down.

"Let's get started." Nathan entered the interrogation room with Gloria following. Mac went to the observation room next door, to watch through the one-way mirror.

Springer, dressed in a suit and tie, sat at the table facing the mirror. He stood when they stepped in.

"Please, sit down," Nathan said. They all sat. "Can we get you anything, coffee, soda, water?"

"No, thank you. I'm fine."

"Mr. Springer, thank you for coming in today. I'm Detective Perry, and you've met Officer Wheeler."

"It's nice to meet you. I want to do whatever I can to help find Ann's killer."

"We appreciate that. Before we begin, we need to read you your rights," Nathan said.

"Wait, you think I had something to do with her death?" Springer asked.

"Not necessarily, but we have to question everyone close to Ann. I assure you, it's just routine." Nathan nodded for Gloria to begin.

Once she finished, she asked, "Do you understand your rights as I have read them to you?"

"Yes," Springer replied.

"Do you wish to have an attorney present for your questioning?"

"No, I have nothing to hide."

"Let's begin," Nathan said. "Do you know where you were on the night of Ann's murder?"

"I worked late at the jewelry store that night and went straight home. I was there all night."

"Can someone from the jewelry store confirm the time that you left?"

"Mr. Judson, the owner, was there when I left. He and I walked out together and he locked up the store."

Nathan wrote that down. "Is there anyone that can verify what time you got home, and that you were there all night?"

Springer thought for a few seconds. "No one stopped by, and I doubt any of my neighbors would remember that specific night."

"Why do you say that?" Gloria asked.

"It was a regular night. Nothing happened in the neighborhood that would help anyone remember it."

He was a smart man. Nathan wasn't sure if that helped or hurt him as a suspect. "How did you and Ann meet?"

"At the jewelry store where I work. She came in to buy a necklace."

"Did she buy one?" Gloria asked.

"Yes. She bought a beautiful ruby necklace."

Gloria and Nathan looked at each other. "I don't suppose the jewelry store would have a photo of that necklace?" Nathan asked.

"I don't know about the jewelry store, but I have a photo of it."

"Why do you have a photo?" Gloria asked.

Springer took out his phone. Scrolling through the photos, he stopped on one. "I have a photo of Ann wearing it." He showed them his phone.

"Could you send that to my phone?" Nathan asked.

Springer handed Nathan his phone. "You can do it yourself."

He took the phone and texted the photo to his phone. "Thanks. How long after you met Ann did you start dating?" Nathan asked.

"I called her a few days later to make sure she was happy with her purchase. We talked for a long time and I ended up asking her out for dinner."

"Does the jewelry store normally do follow-up calls after purchases?"

Springer let out a deep breath. "No. It was an excuse for me to call her. She was a beautiful woman and I wanted to get to know her."

Nathan finished jotting something down before asking the next question. "How long did you two date?"

"Our first date was at the end of February. We broke up the following August."

"Why the breakup?" Gloria asked.

Springer intertwined his fingers, resting his arms on the table. "It was the witchcraft thing. I hated that she was involved in it. You know she was writing articles about it for a cult newspaper in Boston?"

"We know," Nathan said. "When did you find out about it?"

He leaned back in his chair. "She told me about the articles about a month after we started dating. She said that's why she was working at the witchcraft store. It wasn't bad at first, but it slowly started taking over her life. She started spending more time with her Wicca friends than with me. She really started believing in that stuff."

"Do you know Isabella Osborne?"

"She was Ann's boss. I saw her when I would sometimes pick Ann up when she got off work. We never actually met. I always waited for Ann in my car."

"Did you also know Elizabeth Howe?"

"Yes. She lived in the same apartment complex. She stopped by Ann's a few times when I was there, and she had dinner with us once. I barely got a word in that night. All they wanted to talk about were spells and rituals. I ended up going home early. I'm not even sure they knew when I left."

"That must have made you angry," Nathan said.

"Angry? No, but it made me evaluate our relationship."

"How long before you two split up?"

"It was about a month later," Springer said.

"What happened?" Gloria asked.

His expression went sad, and he stared out into space,

rapidly blinking his eyes. "We hadn't been getting along well. We went out to a restaurant for dinner one night. As usual, the conversation led its way to witchcraft." Suddenly, his tone changed to anger. "That witchcraft shit consumed her life. It was all she wanted to talk about. She never asked me about my day." He paused, letting out a deep breath before continuing. "Anyway, she starting talking about her next article for that paper. I tried to talk her out of both the witch stuff and writing those articles. We started getting a little loud, so we left the restaurant." He lowered his head, and spoke faintly. "On the drive home, we argued, and ended our relationship that night. We didn't speak to each other again after that."

Nathan took a few more notes, giving Springer time to compose himself. "Other than Elizabeth Howe and Isabella Osborne, did you ever meet any of her other Wiccan friends?"

"No. She never introduced me to any of the others. She knew how I felt about them."

"How did you feel?" Gloria asked.

"Like I said, I didn't like that stuff."

"Did Ann ever talk about anyone bothering her?" Nathan asked.

Springer thought for a few seconds. She once said she didn't like her apartment manager. He was always asking her out. She called him creepy."

Nathan turned to Gloria. "We talked to the apartment manager, didn't we?"

"Yes, Nick Jones," she replied.

"That was his name," Springer said. "Ann said one time when she and Elizabeth were leaving together, he stopped them, suggesting a threesome."

"What did she do?" Nathan asked.

Springer smiled. "She told me she punched him."

There was a knock at the door. Gloria opened it and stepped out of the room.

He continued. "She also said her editor in Boston made

a pass at her once. She told him she wasn't interested, and it ended with that."

Nathan made a note of those interactions. "Did she ever talk about what went on at the coven meetings?"

"I don't think so…maybe. I'm not sure. I usually tuned her out when she started talking about that."

Gloria came back in and sat down. Nathan looked at her. "Anything wrong?"

"No. Mr. Springer, you cared for Ann very much, even after the breakup, didn't you?"

"Yes, I did."

"If that's true, then why didn't you attend her funeral?" Gloria asked.

His eyes widened after hearing her question. "I visited the funeral home the night before the funeral to say goodbye. I waited until the family had left and the funeral home was about to close. I didn't know any of her family, and never wanted to talk about them. I didn't feel like explaining to them who I was. There would be too many questions."

Nathan took a few seconds to think before proceeding. "Do you still work at Judson's?"

"Yes."

Nathan looked at a page in the case file. "And, you still live at 2041 Dogwood Lane?"

"Yes, I do."

"I think we have all we need for now. If you plan to leave town for anything, please notify us. Thank you for coming in." Nathan got up, followed by Gloria and Springer.

"That's all? You know I didn't hurt Ann, right?" Springer asked.

"We'll be in touch." Nathan and Gloria, followed by Springer, stepped out into the hallway where another officer was waiting. "Officer Stephens, would you escort Mr. Springer to the lobby?"

Once Springer was around the corner, Nathan turned to Gloria. "How did you know he wasn't at the funeral?"

"I told her." Mac was standing next to the observation room door. "That was me that knocked on the door."

"I was just about to ask him about the funeral," Nathan said.

"I didn't know if you'd remember."

"I had the list of names in the case file. The same list you gave." Nathan noticed the officers in the hallway were looking at them.

"If you don't need me for anything else, I'm going back to work," Gloria said.

"Sure. Thanks, Gloria. I need to get back to work too," he said.

Mac followed him to his office. "What the hell is wrong with you today?"

"What are you talking about? Nothing is wrong with me." He sat at his desk, and started looking through the drawers for something, yet looking for nothing.

"You jumped my ass earlier because I was talking about your girlfriend."

Nathan looked up at her.

"Who isn't your girlfriend, and just now, you blew up at me in front of your officers."

Nathan stopped what he was doing, and looked up at Mac. "I'm sorry. This case is driving me crazy. I'm getting nowhere."

Mac sat down. "You don't think Brian Springer might have committed a crime of passion?"

"Do you?" he asked back.

"I don't know either."

"I need to check his alibi with the store owner to see when he left that night. I'll send an officer to talk to his neighbors, and see what we can find out."

"Maybe you need a break. Take the rest of the day off. Do whatever you do to relax. What do you do to relax?" she asked.

"Remember what I said, don't bring up my personal life

at work?" he reminded her.

She threw her hands up in front of her. "I get it. Sorry."

He looked at his watch. "You're right about needing a break. I think I'll go to lunch. Want to go?"

"I can't. I have an online meeting with my office back in Foxborough. I like to keep up to date on the cases my staff are working on. I should get to my computer."

Mac walked out of his office, and Nathan picked up the phone, punching in the number for Dana at work.

"Dana Tyler," she answered.

"Hi, it's Nathan. Busy?"

"What a surprise. Not too busy."

He could hear her typing as she talked. "If it's not a good time, I can call back."

"I'm just finishing up a story for tomorrow's edition. Did you need something?"

"Would you like to meet for lunch?"

"Yes. That would be nice," she said.

"Great. Is the Witch's Brew okay?"

"Sounds good to me."

"I'll see you there in a few minutes then."

"I really need to finish this article first. Give me about ten minutes to get it done, and I'll head over," she said.

"I'll head over and grab a table."

They both hung up. Nathan decided to walk to the café. He let the officers at the front desk know he was leaving for lunch as he walked through the lobby.

A short walk down the street, he entered the Witch's Brew Café. Busy, as usual, he found a booth by the window overlooking the street. He waved at Ginger as he slid into the side of the booth where he could see the front door.

A few minutes after he sat down, Ginger came over with a soda for him. "How's your day going?" she asked.

"Not the best I've had." He took a drink of the soda.

"Typical day, eh? What can I get you today?" she asked.

"I'm meeting Dana. I'll wait for her, but she'll probably

want an iced tea."

"I'll bring it over when I see her come in." Ginger headed back to the counter.

Nathan took a small notepad out of his coat pocket and wrote down some questions to ask Springer's boss. He heard the bell on the door chime, and saw Dana walk in. She headed to the table after seeing Nathan wave.

"I hope I'm not too late," she said, sitting across from him.

"Not at all. I've only been here a few minutes."

Ginger approached the table with a glass of iced tea. "The stud here ordered you a tea."

"That's perfect. Thanks, Ginger." Dana tore open a yellow packet of artificial sweetener, stirring it into the drink.

"What can I bring you two?" Ginger asked.

"Vegetable soup for me," Dana said.

"I'll take a BLT and fries," Nathan added.

"It'll be right out." She took the orders to the kitchen.

Dana took a sip of her tea. "Busy morning?"

"I was in an interrogation most of the morning."

"Anything you can tell me about?"

"I wish I could, but I can't, not yet. There's too much to check out before I can make a statement."

"Yeah, I know. I had to ask, though. It's the job," she said.

"As is mine." He took a drink of his soda.

"Oh, I do have something to tell you, but you can't reveal me as your source," he said.

"Reporter's code; I promise."

"A woman in Salem was found burned at the stake. She was a practicing witch," he said.

"No kidding? Do you think it's related to the murders here?"

"I can't say anything else. Sorry."

"I understand. I'll call the Salem PD today."

"Just don't mention my name. I don't want them to know I leaked this to you."

"I promise."

"What story were you working on when I called?" he asked.

"Actually, it's a companion article to the murders. I was writing an article about witchcraft." She took a sip of her tea from the straw.

"Are you sure that's a good idea?"

"Why wouldn't it be? It's very timely with the murders, and since it's October, it fits in nicely."

"Just be careful and watch your back. There's still a murderer on the loose," he said,

Ginger walked up, arms loaded with plates. "Here you go." She placed the food in front of them. "Can I get you anything else?"

"I'm good."

"Me, too," Dana added.

"Give me a shout, if you need something." She walked to the next table to take their order.

Nathan took a bite of his sandwich.

"Oh, I almost forgot. I have some news," Dana said.

Nathan swallowed. "What's your news?"

"I've been appointed to the Board of Directors of the Mystic Public Library."

"That's wonderful. Congratulations." He reached over to give her hand a squeeze.

"Thanks. It's not that exciting, or anything like that. But, Mrs. Olsen, the librarian, has said she's going to retire in the next year or two, so I'll have input in choosing her replacement."

"I've met Mrs. Olsen. She helped me find some books on coin collecting when I investigated the coin convention murder. She made me get a library card before she'd let me take the books."

"That's her job. I bet you haven't read a book from there since, have you?"

"My job really doesn't leave much time for reading."

Dana laughed. "Excuses, excuses." Nathan laughed too.

At that moment, his phone rang. "Sorry." He looked at the display. "It's work. Perry."

"Nathan, it's Gloria. Detective Jennings from the Salem PD called. They found Isabella Osborne's car in Salem."

"Did they process it for evidence yet?"

"They did once they realized it was involved in an assault case. They want us to come and get it."

"Do we still use Bill's Towing?"

"Yes."

"I'll head back to the office in just a bit and will return the detective's call." He closed his phone.

"Problem?" Dana asked.

"I have to go." Nathan put some money on the table to cover their bill.

"And, you can't talk about it? It sounded interesting."

"Sorry, but no. I'll call you later." He took one more bite of his sandwich, then left the café.

Gloria was dealing with a resident when Nathan walked through the lobby, so he went straight to his office. A few minutes later, she was at his door.

"I meant to catch you when you came in, but Mr. Jackson was in complaining about his neighbor again. Here's the contact information for the detective in Salem." She handed him a pink message sheet.

"Did he say anything other than come and get the car?"

"Only what I already told you. I put Bill's Towing number on the back of the paper."

"I'm probably going to drive up there. I need for you to do something for me today while I'm gone."

"Of course. What do you need?" She sat down.

"I was going to talk to Brian Springer's boss today to corroborate his alibi. Could you go see Mr. Judson for me? I'll clear it with Sergeant Donnelly."

"I'd be glad to," she said.

Nathan tore a page out of his notepad. "Here's some of

the questions I was going to ask. You can improvise the rest as you go."

"I'll have Cindy cover for me up front." She took the paper from him and left the office.

After a thirty minute drive to Salem, Nathan sat across the desk from Detective John Jennings. "I appreciate you calling us right away after finding the car," Nathan said.

"We just want to help in any way we can," Jennings replied.

"That's good to hear, because I think the person who stole that car may have been responsible for your recent case of the woman burned at the stake."

"Detective Denzinger dropped off a copy of your case files to me earlier today. After reading through them, I think you're right."

"He gave me a copy of your file as well, but I only had time to glance at it. Do you have any suspects?"

"None. It makes no sense. It's been over three-hundred years since a witch was burned in Salem. Do you think it's a vigilante, or just a crazy serial killer?" Jennings asked.

"I don't know, maybe a little of both. Other than the witchcraft thing, none of my victims had any other connections to each other."

"It looked like you have several suspects though."

"Yes, but I can't prove any of them did it."

"Seems like that's how it goes, doesn't it? I assume you'll share whatever you find with me?"

"Of course," Nathan said. "And, you with me?"

"I will." Jennings phone buzzed. He pushed the speaker button. "Yes."

"Detective, the tow truck driver from the Mystic PD is here for that car. Can we release it?" the officer asked.

"Yes, you can release it. Their detective is with me now. "I'll bring him down to the garage."

****

Gloria pushed the door open at Judson's Jewelry Store and entered. It appeared to be a slow day. She saw only one customer in the store full of display cases of watches, necklaces, rings, and just about any type of jewelry you could think of. She did not see Brian Springer anywhere.

A young lady approached. "May I help you, officer?"

"I'm Gloria Wheeler from the Mystic Police Department. I'd like to speak to Mr. Judson. Is he here?"

"Yes. He's in his office. Let me check with him. It'll only take a moment." The sales clerk disappeared at the rear of the store.

Gloria looked down at the display of earrings and necklaces that probably cost way more than her pay grade. "A lady can dream," she quietly said to herself.

"Officer Wheeler, if you'll come with me. Mr. Judson will see you." The young lady had reappeared, then led Gloria to an office.

When she entered, an older, partially bald gentleman slowly stood. "Officer Wheeler, please come in. I'm Elias Judson." They shook hands, and Judson motioned for her to sit.

"Thank you for seeing me, Mr. Judson. I'm here about one of your employees, Brian Springer."

"Brian? What about him?"

"We're trying to confirm his whereabouts on the night of September twenty-third," Gloria said.

"What? What do you think he's done?" Judson looked confused.

"I'm here to try and clear up any suspicion we have. Could you tell me what time he left work that night?"

"Certainly." He rolled his chair closer to the computer at the side of his desk, and started typing. The screen changed and Judson stared at it. "I remember that day. He and I closed the store together that night. It was at six-o'clock."

Gloria wrote in her notebook. "You're sure about that time?"

"It's right here on his time sheet." He pointed to the monitor.

"Could I get a copy of his time sheet for that week?"

Judson clicked his mouse and a paper came out of the printer. He handed it to her.

"How do you remember that night?" she asked.

He rolled his chair back to his desk. "It was my anniversary. I had hoped to leave early to take my wife to dinner, but we were very busy that day. I had to stay until closing. We missed our dinner reservation." He smiled. "My wife ended up having dinner delivered, and we dined by candlelight in our own house. It was actually better than eating out."

"That sounds nice. Did you ever meet Mr. Springer's girlfriend, Ann Parker?"

"The young lady that was murdered? So, that's what this is about. Yes, I met her a couple times when she came in to meet him for a date. She was a nice girl," Judson said.

"How did they interact together?"

"Do you think Brian had something to do with her murder? He worshiped her. He was devasted when she ended their relationship."

Gloria looked up in surprise. "She broke up with him?" This was the opposite of what Springer said at his interview.

"Yes. That's what he told me. I felt bad for him. The few times I saw them together, they looked like a lovely couple. What happened to her was so tragic."

"It certainly was. I didn't see Mr. Springer in the store. Is he here today?" she asked.

"He called in this morning to say he wouldn't be in today."

"Did he say why?"

"No, and I didn't ask. He rarely misses work. If he needed to take a day off, I didn't mind. I assumed he had a good reason."

Gloria finished jotting down the last of her notes. "I think I'm finished." She stood. "Thank you for your time, Mr. Judson."

"You're welcome. If I can be of any more help, please let me know." Judson stood as Gloria left his office.

Back in her car, she felt uneasy about Springer not being at work today. Her copy of the case file was on the seat next to her. She decided she needed to check on Springer. After finding his address in the file, she drove to his neighborhood.

When she turned onto his street, she was surprised to see him standing in his yard, holding a rake, and talking to someone, likely a neighbor. Gloria really wanted to stop and ask him why he didn't go back to work after his questioning this morning, but technically, she didn't have cause to do that. She drove past his house, heading back to the police department.

Chapter Eleven

Nathan entered the garage where Isabella's car was housed. He found it on the far side of the large building. All four doors and the trunk were open, but no one seemed to be around.

"Mallory, are you here?" he shouted.

A head popped up through one of the door windows. "I'm here," she replied, waving her hand.

He walked over to the side of the car, where he found her on her knees looking under the seats. "I thought Salem's CSU already went over the car."

"They did." Wearing baggy blue coveralls, she stood. "I want to make sure they didn't miss anything."

"Did they?"

"No. They did a good job. Come over here and I'll show you what they did find." Nathan followed Mallory to a metal cabinet against the wall. She unlocked it, taking out a brown envelope. From it, she pulled out an evidence bag, handing it to Nathan.

He held the clear plastic bag up in front of him. "Candy wrappers."

"Not just any candy wrappers, but the same type of wrappers that we found at Ann Parker's crime scene."

He looked at the evidence again. "I'll be damn. This is the connection we've been looking for. What about DNA from the wrappers?"

"I'll send them to the State Crime Lab today to be tested. There wasn't any from the first crime scene, so don't get your hopes up."

"I don't suppose we were lucky enough to find Isabella's emerald amulet in the car?" he asked.

"Sorry. The car had been wiped clean, so no fingerprints either. We were lucky to find the candy wrappers. According to Salem's technician, they were found under the driver's seat. The killer probably didn't realize he'd dropped them."

"It's not much, but at least we know our subject has a sweet tooth." He gave the evidence bag back to Mallory. "Let me know if anything else turns up."

Nathan left the garage, walking across the parking lot back to the police department. About halfway to the building, a pain shot through his leg, the one injured in Afghanistan. He had to catch himself on a car to keep from falling.

Unfortunately, he'd been having this pain more often lately. It only lasted a few seconds, then it was gone. He continued on his way to the building, hoping no one saw him, and trying to hide his limp. Officers were coming out of the morning briefing as Nathan approached his office.

"Just the person I need to see," Gloria said.

He waited to see if she was going to ask him about what happened in the parking lot.

"I wanted to fill you in on my interview with Mr. Judson."

He turned to unlock his office door. A wave of relief passed through him. "Come on in."

They went in and sat down. Gloria explained everything she learned from Judson, giving Nathan the copy of Springer's time sheet for the week of Ann's murder. Then, they were interrupted.

"Excuse me, sir."

"Officer Walker, what do you have for me?" Nathan said.

He entered. "Hi, Gloria."

"James."

"Detective, I spoke with Brian Springer's neighbors, like you asked. I emailed you my report, sir."

"It was obvious to Nathan that Walker was nervous talking to him. "Relax, James. It's just police work."

The young officer smiled; his body relaxing a little.

"Did you have any trouble with the neighbors?" Nathan asked.

"No, sir. They asked why I needed to know, but seemed satisfied with my saying I couldn't elaborate. They all remembered that night because they were having a neighborhood party, and they all remembered Springer being there. They said it was pretty much an all-night party."

"That clears Springer then," Gloria said.

"Not exactly," Walker replied.

"What do you mean, not exactly?" Nathan asked.

"You'll see the neighbors' statements in my report, but basically, they all remember seeing him that night, but no one could pinpoint the times.

"He could have been seen, left to kill her, and then returned to the neighborhood to be seen again later," Gloria said.

Nathan blew out a deep breath. "That's exactually what he could have done." He leaned back in his chair. "Damn it." Frustration was getting the better of him.

"If you don't need me for anything else, I should get on patrol," Walker said.

"Sure. Thanks for your help, James. You did a good job. I'll make sure to email Sergeant Donnelly about your work."

"Thank you, sir." Walker left.

"Funny Springer didn't mention the neighborhood party. In fact, I believe he said it was a regular night with nothing much going on. I would think a party like that would be worth mentioning, especially if it cleared you as a murder suspect."

"I think so too. What's next?" Gloria asked.

"Is Hank working today?"

"No. He pulled the second shift. He'll be in around three."

Nathan flipped though the pages of the case file until he found what he wanted. He pushed the speaker button on his desk phone, and punched in the number.

"Parker residence."

"Detective Perry calling for William Parker."

"One moment, Detective."

He heard the receiver being placed on the table. A few minutes later, the phone was picked up.

"This is William Parker. What can I do for you, Detective Perry?"

"Mr. Parker, I would like to speak to you again. This time in an official capacity. When can you come to Mystic?" Nathan could hear mumbling, as if he were covering the receiver with his hand. "Mr. Parker?"

"Yes, I'm still here. What do you mean by an official capacity?"

Nathan looked at Gloria, smiling. "What I mean is I will be questioning you about your daughter's murder...officially, as in it will be recorded."

Again, more muffled talking.

"If you want to talk to me, you'll have to do it at my home. You'll have to arrest me, if you want me in Mystic."

"One moment, Mr. Parker." Nathan put the call on hold. "Someone is advising him," he said to Gloria.

"But, who? He didn't know you were going to call."

Nathan went back onto the call. "I'll be at your house in ninety-minutes." He ended the call.

"You didn't let him answer."

"I didn't want him to tell me no."

I'd be happy to accompany you," she offered.

"I can do this one myself. I have something else for you. Do you know how to fill out a warrant request?"

"I've never done it, but I've seen plenty of them."

"I need for you to request a warrant for William Parker's financial records, including bank accounts and credit report," he said. "Have Sergeant Donnelly look it over before you take it to the district attorney. I'll call Daniel Grant, so he'll be expecting it, and hopefully he can get a judge to sign it right away."

"I'll get right on it." She started to get up.

"I'm not finished. While you're waiting for the warrant, do a background check on Parker. Don't forget to search for a criminal record too. Then, when the warrant comes in, get the financials on him. I want to know more about him than his wife knows."

"I won't let you down."

"Good. I'll call the D.A., then get on the road."

Gloria left, and Nathan made his phone call before leaving for Foxborough.

As he drove up to the Parker home, he saw several very expensive cars parked in the driveway. Patrick, the butler, answered the door, then led him into the den where Mr. Parker sat behind his desk. His brother-in-law, Father Michael Dunbar, sat on the couch, and two men, who Nathan didn't know, were standing near the window.

"Detective Perry, welcome to my home," Parker said.

Nathan stepped into the room. "Thank you for meeting with me today."

"You didn't leave me much choice," Parker replied. "I believe you know Father Mike. He'll be my spiritual advisor today."

Nathan wondered why Parker needed spiritual support. "It's nice to see you again, Father."

The priest nodded to Nathan.

"Detective Perry," one of the other gentlemen said. "I'm Edward Bell, one of Mr. Parker's attorneys. This is my associate, Joseph Turner."

"How do you do, Detective Perry?" Turner said.

"It's nice to meet you," Nathan responded. Parker, didn't waste any time lawyering up. "Shall we get started? Mr. Parker, let's sit around the coffee table." He wanted to get Parker out from behind the desk. It was too much of a power position, and Nathan wanted to be on equal ground.

Bell nodded slightly to Parker, who stood and moved to a chair at one end of the table. Father Mike stood, letting Bell and Turner sit on the couch, with him moving to the chair behind Parker.

"This is just preliminary questioning, but I will be recording it." Nathan sat down opposite Parker, placing a digital audio recorder on the coffee table. "I'm terrible at taking notes." He wanted to appear a bit inept, sort of a Columbo approach to questioning, so hopefully Parker would slip up with his answers.

"Will a copy of the recording be available to us?" Turner asked.

"Not at this time, but you're welcome to make your own recording. If you feel it's necessary, later I can have a transcript sent to you, at your expense, of course."

"William, do you have a recorder?" Bell asked.

"No, I don't. Father Mike?"

"What would I do with something like that?"

"Shall we get started then? I will be reading you your rights once we go on the record." Nathan pushed a button on the recorder, and began. "For the record, this is Detective Nathan Perry, also present are William Parker, his attorneys Edward Bell and Joseph Turner, and Father Michael Dunbar, Mr. Parker's brother-in-law and spiritual advisor. Mr. Parker, at this time, I will be reading you your rights." Once he finished, Parker agreed to talk since his attorneys were present.

Mr. Turner sat with a yellow legal pad taking notes, while the other attorney prepared to listen.

Nathan began. "Mr. Parker, in a previous discussion we had, you said you didn't know Ann's whereabouts until her body was found. Is that still your statement?"

"It is. I had no idea where she was after she moved out of our home in November."

"Are you sure you want to stick with that story?" Nathan asked.

"What are you getting at, Detective?" Bell asked.

"What I'm getting at is that Mr. Parker is lying."

"How dare you accuse me of lying," Parker said.

"William," Bell said, holding his hand up to Parker.

"Mr. Parker, the bank manager at the Mystic State Bank said your bank called there wanting your daughter's address. You knew she was in Mystic, but you told me you didn't. What else are you hiding?"

"Don't answer that, William," Bell interrupted. "It sounds like you're accusing him of having something to do with Ann's murder."

"I'm doing my best to rule him out, but it's difficult to do when I discover he's lied to me."

"Detective," Parker said.

"William, don't say anything," Bell advised.

Parker ignored his attorney. "I never asked my bank to find Ann's address."

He seemed sincere, but Nathan was still skeptical. "Do you realize finding out that you knew she was in Mystic threw up all kinds of red flags."

"I appreciate you not giving up on finding my daughter's killer," Parker said.

Nathan was astounded that Parker still played the grieving father.

"Do you have any other suspects?" Father Mike asked.

"We do. We're investigating everyone involved with her."

"Detective, unless you plan on filing some sort of charges against Mr. Parker, I'm going to have to end this questioning," Bell said.

"Very well. I appreciate your time," Nathan said. He picked up the recorder from the table, then turned to leave. Stopping, he turned back toward the men. "I have one more question. Why didn't you have your private investigator find Ann's address?"

"I did. Mac Dupont is the one who found her. Didn't she tell you?" Parker asked.

Nathan felt like the breath had been knocked out of him. "No, she didn't. When did she find her?"

She discovered her whereabouts in February," Parker said.

Nathan was speechless. He turned to leave, but noticed something on the table next to the hallway door, a bowl of hard candy. Mixed in with the various types of candy were pieces of peppermint candy that matched the wrappers found at Ann's murder scene and in Isabella's car. He looked back at Parker, "May I?" He pointed to the candy bowl.

Parker looked more annoyed, than anything, but gave Nathan a "whatever" look, raising his hand.

He took that as a yes, and picked out two pieces of the peppermint candy. He placed them in his coat pocket, and followed Patrick to the front door. Once he reached his car, he turned off the digital recorder he held in his hand. He didn't want to miss anything that might have been said after they thought the recorder was off. Before driving away, he put the two pieces of candy into an evidence bag, writing the time and place they were from on the bag.

Nathan left the Parker property, heading toward the highway. He was furious to find out that Mac had concealed information. He needed a drink. Bypassing his exit, he turned around, driving to the downtown area of Foxborough.

A short time later, he walked into the bar where David Anders worked. Sure, it was the middle of a weekday, but Nathan found Anders standing behind the bar working. He took a seat near him.

"What can I get you?" Anders automatically asked, without looking at Nathan.

"Just a beer."

Anders then looked up. "What do you want?"

"I just said a beer."

Anders filled a tall glass from the beer on tap, sitting it in front of Nathan. "You know what I mean. You're going to get me fired," he quietly said.

"Take it easy. No one will know who I am or why I'm here, unless you make a scene." Nathan took a drink of his beer.

"How did you know I'd be here today? My hours changed."

"I needed a drink, and took a chance."

"So, you found me. What are you here for?" Anders asked.

Nathan took another drink of his beer, but before he could answer, a waitress called for Anders from the end of the bar. He walked down there to get the drinks she needed. That's when Nathan saw the large container of peppermint candy next to the cash register; the same peppermint candy.

Anders stepped back to Nathan. "You didn't answer me."

"Have you come up with an alibi for that night yet?"

"How can I come up with an alibi when I was home by myself?"

"I thought maybe you had found a neighbor that might have seen you," Nathan said.

"You guys already talked to my neighbors. Thanks to that, they give me a wide berth when I meet them in the hall."

"We were just doing our job." He took another drink of his beer. "What's with the big jug of candy there?" Nathan pointed to the candy jar.

Anders turned toward the candy, and then back to Nathan. "Some customers don't like alcohol on their breath when they leave the bar."

Nathan stood and took out his wallet. "I'll take a couple of them."

Anders got two pieces of the candy and put them on the bar in front of Nathan, who threw some money on the counter for his beer and candy.

He picked up the two pieces. "Thanks. Keep the change," Nathan said before leaving the bar. When he got into his car, he did the same as at the Parker house, putting the candy in an evidence bag, and labeling it.

****

It was late that afternoon when Nathan returned back in Mystic. He went straight to see Mallory, who was sitting at her desk. "Hi, Mallory. I've got some evidence I need for you to examine."

"Sure. Have a seat. Let's see what you've got."

He handed her both evidence bags.

"What's this?" She took the bags.

"Candy in wrappers like the ones found at Ann's crime and Isabella's car. Can you match those to the wrappers we have?"

"Maybe."

"Maybe?"

"They're candy wrappers. Sure, they're from the same company, but that company wraps thousands of these mints a day. I'll log these in as evidence, but that's the best I can do."

Frustrated, Nathan let out a deep breath. "Go ahead and log them in. Hopefully, we'll get lucky."

She took the bags, and started typing on her computer.

"Have you seen Mac Dupont today?" he asked.

"I've barely been out of my office today. I'm sorry. I don't know if she's here, or not."

"Thanks anyway." Nathan left her office, and walked to the front desk to find Gloria.

She turned around as he walked toward her. "How was your interview with Mr. Parker?" she asked.

"Informative. Very informative. Is Chief Cabot in today?"

"Yes, he should be in his office."

Nathan started to walk away. "Wait, don't you want to hear about Parker's financials?" she asked.

"I do, but I need to talk to the chief first." He left the lobby, walking to elevator at the rear of the building. With his leg acting up, he didn't want to take a chance on the stairs. He pushed the button for the second floor.

When he got off the elevator, he rounded the corner,

and stood in the chief's doorway. "Excuse me, Chief Cabot. Do you have a minute? I have a situation I need to talk to you about."

"Perry, yes, come in." Nathan stepped into the office and sat in front of the chief's desk. "I haven't seen you much lately. I wondered if you still worked here."

"I very much work here, sir. I've been away from the office investigating our murders. That's what I came to talk to you about today. I've uncovered some disturbing news." Nathan tried to stay calm, but he was becoming angrier by the minute.

"Well, go on. You look like you're about to explode."

He took a deep breath and let it out slowly, before beginning. "I discovered William Parker, the father of the first murder victim, lied about knowing his daughter was living here. He got that information from a private investigator he hired to find her. That P.I. was Mac Dupont."

"The woman downstairs who has been assisting with the investigation?"

"Yes, sir." Nathan stood. He needed to pace to expend some of his pent-up anger. "She never revealed this information, and has had access to all of the case files. For all we know, she could be reporting everything back to Mr. Parker, who is one of my prime suspects."

Nathan could see the chief's face turn red. "Get that woman out of this building, and don't let her take any case files with her," Chief Cabot ordered.

"Yes, sir. Thank you." Nathan quickly left the office.

Several minutes later, he stood at Mac's office door with Sergeant Donnelly, Officer Avery, and Mallory.

"What's this, a party?' Mac asked.

"Not exactly," Nathan said. "Mallory and the officers are here to go through your computer and paper files to remove any case information found as a result of the police investigation into the witch murders. I'm here to question you."

"Question me? What are you talking about?"

"If you'll accompany me to the interrogation room, I'll explain."

Mac followed Nathan out into the hallway, while Mallory and the two officers went into her office to collect any material to stay at the police department.

Officer Cindy Walker stood waiting for them at the door of the interrogation room. She opened the door and stepped in, followed by Mac and Nathan. Closing the door, Officer Walker stood by the door.

Mac sat down. "What am I supposed to have done?"

Nathan took the seat across the table. "Mr. Parker told me today that he knew Ann was in Mystic because you found out she was living here. Did you just sort of forget to mention that while you were presumably helping me with the investigation? I ought to arrest you for withholding evidence."

"Then, why don't you?" Mac snapped back.

"Because, I don't want to look at you any longer than I have to. You disgust me. I hate to think what kind of officer you were with the Boston PD."

"I was a damn good officer," she shouted back.

Not wanting to get into a shouting match, Nathan took a deep breath, letting it out to calm down. "What did you do with the information you learned from my investigation?"

"I didn't do anything with it. None of it left the building."

"Why were you really here?"

"I'm here to help find Ann Parker's killer."

"Or, are you here to lead me away from her father as the killer?"

"What can I do to convince you to the otherwise?" she asked.

The door opened. Mallory and Sergeant Donnelly walked in.

"Did you find anything?" Nathan asked.

"We've packed up all the hard copies from her office to go through in the evidence room," Sergeant Donnelly said.

"I erased all the files from her computer, and cleaned the hard drive," Mallory said.

Mac stood up. "You wiped my hard drive? I had important files on there." She looked at Nathan. "My files, not yours."

"Sit down," he ordered.

She did as she was told.

Mallory continued, "I also checked the sent folder to see if she emailed any files. I didn't find anything. However, I couldn't get into her phone." She held up Mac's smart phone.

"You can't just go through my files," Mac said.

"Yes, we can. You're working under us, in this building, and on our Wi-Fi. Remember signing an internet agreement when you first got your office? There was a stack of forms you signed, two of which relinquished your rights to privacy for any personal devices used in this building. That includes your phone, and also gives us the right to erase your hard drive." Nathan took the phone from Mallory. He held it out to Mac. "Unlock it."

Reluctantly, Mac unlocked her phone, handing it back to Nathan, who then gave it to Mallory. She and Sergeant Donnelly left the room.

Just as they went out, Officer Avery appeared at the door. "Everything's all boxed up, and being moved to the evidence room."

"Good. Do you have your wallet and car keys with you?" Nathan asked Mac.

"Yes, in my pocket."

"Officer Walker and Officer Avery, would you escort Miss Dupont to her car, and make sure she drives off the property?"

"What about my phone and laptop?" she asked.

"We'll send them to you. Oh, and I'll be filing a report with the Massachusetts Licensing Bureau asking them to pull your private investigator license," Nathan said. "Now, get the hell out of this building."

"I want to talk to Chief Cabot. He'd never allow this."

"Chief Cabot is the one who ordered it." Nathan nodded

to the officers, who then led Mac out of the room. Now, alone and angry, Nathan sat back down to take a few moments to himself. It didn't last long.

The door flew open. "Thank God, I found you," Gloria said, rushing into the room.

"I actually was hoping for a little quiet time," he said.

"There's no time for that. Elizabeth Howe's car has been found."

Nathan perked right up. "What? Where? Who found it?"

"A fishing boat crew spotted a car in Mystic Hollow Bay. They called 911, and we sent a dive team down there. When they ran the plate, they got a hit on Elizabeth's car. Hank is down there right now questioning the boat crew."

"I'm going to head out there. Do you want to come?"

"I'm going off duty in a few minutes, but if you can wait until I call my husband to tell him I'll be late getting home, I'll go with you," she said.

"You do that, and I'll pull the car out front to pick you up."

"That sounds like a plan." They both left the room.

Nathan was parked out in front of the police department when Gloria came out. She got in and buckled up.

"Did your husband mind you being late tonight?" Nathan asked.

"No. It's still football season, and he has practice again tonight. I'll pick something up for dinner from the Witch's Brew on the way home."

Mystic Hollow Bay, located on the north side of Mystic, is an inlet area from the ocean. When they arrived, they saw flashing lights from the police cars already on the scene. Bill's Towing was already there too. Nathan parked the car, and he and Gloria walked over to Hank.

"Anything yet?" Nathan asked.

"The divers just hooked up the tow cable, it shouldn't be long now," Hank said.

One of the divers popped through the surface of the

water, giving a thumbs-up signal. The motor on the tow truck fired up. The sound of the grinding gears guaranteed something heavy was coming up.

Mallory, dressed in coveralls and rubber boots, walked up behind the officers. "Looks like I haven't missed anything yet," she said loudly over the sound of the motor.

The officers jumped, not knowing she was there. "Damn, Mal. Announce yourself when you get here," Nathan said, holding his chest.

Mallory laughed. "Next time, I'll hit the siren on the van."

The officers laughed.

"I figured you'd locked all of Mac's stuff up, and left for the day," Nathan said.

"I was just getting ready to leave when the call came in. I didn't want any possible evidence to get compromised, so I headed here."

The car broke through the surface of the water, being pulled closer to the edge. Once it reached solid ground, the tow truck driver shut the motor down. Water leaked from every crevice of the car. Mallory and the officers walked over. She peered inside before doing anything.

"No body inside," she said.

"Did you think there would be?" Gloria asked.

"Not really, but you never know." Mallory started putting down what looked like a flat fishing net on the ground, along one side of the car. "Everyone, stand back. I'm going to open the door."

By now, the divers had come out of the water and stood behind the car. Mallory asked them to be ready to catch anything from the car that the net might miss. With everyone else away from the car, she grasped the door handle.

After a few tugs, the front door opened. It was as if a dam had broken. Water poured out of the car, along with several items caught by the net.

Once the water stopped flowing, she opened the back door. The rush of water wasn't as swift as the front door, but a few more things came out in the stream, and were caught by the net.

Nathan, Hank, and Gloria walked over to the car to see what had come out. Mallory was kneeling down, putting items in a bucket.

"Anything interesting?" Nathan asked.

Mallory held up her hand with candy wrappers in it. "I'll get these sent to the lab tomorrow for DNA analysis, but I doubt we'll get a hit."

"Anything else?"

"I'll need to pump out the rest of the water from the floor, and also the trunk, before the car can be moved. It's going to be dark soon. I'll need some help setting up some lights," she said, heading to her van.

"I can stay here with Mallory," Hank said. Another officer volunteered to stay also.

Nathan looked around. A small group of onlookers had gathered. "I'm going to take Gloria back to town, and I'll radio in to make sure we have enough officers out here for crowd control."

"You don't have to take me back. I can stay here to help," Gloria said.

"No. I don't want you working any more off the clock," Nathan said. "You need to get home, and so do I. It's been a long, stressful day, and I need a beer." He turned to Hank. "Call me, if you find anything important."

Nathan and Gloria walked back to his car, and drove back to town.

After dropping Gloria off at her car, Nathan went inside the police department to lock the case file in his desk before going home. He sat at his desk putting documents and photos into the file. Lastly, he took the digital recorder, from earlier today, out of his pocket.

He really needed to upload the interview, but that would take too long to do. He put the recorder in his desk, along with the case file, and locked the drawer. He started to stand, but noticed the red voicemail light on the desk phone blinking. He pushed the button.

"Mr. Perry, this is Donna from Walter Reed Hospital Orthopedic Department. We received your message about your leg pain. Your checkup exam is coming up in a few months, so your doctor thought we'd go ahead and have you come in as soon as possible to see what is causing the pain. Please call tomorrow to get an appointment scheduled. Thank you."

He deleted the message.

"Nathan, what leg pain is she talking about?" It was Dana standing at his door.

"It's nothing. What are you doing here?"

"I saw your truck out back, and thought I'd see if you wanted to have dinner. What was that message about?" she asked again.

"It's nothing for you to worry about."

"But I am worried."

"It's probably just some arthritis that has set in." He stood. "I'd love to go to dinner, but I've had a long day, and I'm tired. I just want to go home to sleep."

"I know we're not in a relationship, other than an occasional night together, but I care about you. Call for that appointment, and let me know what they say."

He walked her out into the hall, and gave her a kiss on the cheek. "I promise."

She left, walking toward the lobby. Nathan locked his office, leaving by the back door.

Chapter Twelve

Nathan tossed and turned all night, and with little sleep, he finally got up at four a.m. Standing up from his bed, pain shot through his leg so bad he had to sit back down. After a few minutes of massaging his knee, he was able to stand and made his way to the kitchen. He picked up the coffee pot and filled it with water.

Two scrambled eggs and one cup of coffee later, he decided to go ahead into work. He was sitting at his desk, on his fourth cup of coffee, when Gloria stepped in.

"Good morning," she greeted.

"I don't know about good, but morning." He took a drink of his coffee.

"Is this a good time to talk about William Parker's financials and criminal history?"

He perked up. "He has a criminal history?"

"He does, but it was when he was younger. I think you'll find it interesting, though."

"Don't you need to get to this morning's briefing?"

"I'll get a copy from Donnelly later," she answered.

"Sit down and fill me in on Parker then," he said.

"He has a history of domestic violence from forty years ago. The police were called to his home several times by his wife. Apparently, he had a temper."

"Were charges filed?"

"They were, but the court record showed he and his wife were ordered to counseling. Instead of a mental health agency, they went to their priest for the counseling," Gloria said.

"Let me guess. It was Father Mike?"

"No, but close. They went to their own church, of which Father Mike was a member, but another priest tended to them. They completed several weeks of family counseling. With no more reports of violence after that, the charges were dropped." She handed Nathan the report.

He read it over. "Is there any way to check with Child Services to see if there were any abuse reports with Ann?"

"It'll take a court order, but if there were any, it would only show substantiated reports. Anything unsubstantiated would have been purged long ago."

"Contact Daniel Grant for a warrant, and see what you can find." He took another drink of coffee. "What about Parker's financials?"

"He's worth millions," she said.

"I think that's pretty obvious."

"Wow. Sarcasm so early in the morning?"

Nathan leaned forward, elbows on his desk, head in his hands. "I'm sorry." He sat back up. "I didn't sleep well last night. I'm full of coffee, and ...." He stopped mid-sentence, rubbing his leg under the desk.

"And, what?"

"Nothing. Go ahead with your report."

Gloria continued. "Like I said, he's worth millions, but was worth a lot more last year. He lost a lot in the stock market."

"What about his company?"

"From what I could find online, he started downsizing his company several months ago."

"Why?"

"The financial report doesn't tell that," she said.

"But you checked into it, right?"

A smile slowly spread across her face. "Yes."

"I knew it. What did you find?"

"I checked several financial investment web sites. Parker's company has been losing clients to new companies that have been outbidding his company on new jobs. His company's biggest client is still Gillette Stadium, where he holds the contract on their lighting."

"That has to be a huge contract," Nathan said.

"It is, but not enough to sustain the company on its own. The financial report shows he's been selling his own stock in the company. He's also been applying for loans to keep the company going. That's pretty much it. I'll email you a copy of his financials and everything I found for the case file."

"Thanks, Gloria. You've done a wonderful job."

"Do you think he did it because of money?"

"I was concerned that he might be in debt to the wrong people. After seeing your report, I don't think that's the case."

"Why do you think that?" she asked.

"I doubt loan sharks, or the mob, could loan as much money as he needs."

"Can anyone join this party?" State Police Detective Sam Denzinger walked into the office.

"You're welcome anytime," Nathan said. "Coffee?"

"I could use a cup. Good morning, Officer Wheeler." Denzinger sat down.

"Good morning, Detective."

Nathan got up, slowly walking to the coffeemaker on the table behind the door.

"When did you get coffee in here?" Gloria asked.

"I got tired of drinking that -- stuff -- from the breakroom." He handed Denzinger a cup. "Do you want some?" he asked Gloria.

"No, I need to get to work, but now that I know where the good coffee is, expect to see me more often, cup in hand. Detective," she nodded to Denzinger.

"Officer," he responded, as she left.

Nathan sat back down behind his desk. "What brings you here today?" he asked Denzinger.

"I needed a day out of the office, and thought I'd check to see how your witch murders are going."

"It's not going well. I can't help but think I'm missing something. I have suspects, but can't nail any of them directly to the murders, and I have evidence that I can't connect to any of them at all."

"Who are your suspects?"

"All are connected to Ann Parker, the first victim. There's her father, her boyfriend when she left home, the boyfriend she had here in Mystic, and Joe Cassidy. He's the only one that's connected to all the victims.

"He's your man then."

"I'm not sure. He's the only one I know personally. I can't see him being a killer." The intercom buzzed on Nathan's phone. He pushed a button. "Good morning, Mallory."

"There's not much good about it. I have some information on the evidence from the witch's case. If you're not busy, I'll come to your office to go over it," she said.

"Detective Denzinger is here to discuss the case, so it's a perfect time."

"I'll be right there."

Mallory immediately came to Nathan's office, and she took a seat in front of his desk next to Denzinger. Nathan saw her eyeing his coffee as she sat down. "Would you like some coffee?" he asked.

She shuddered. "I can't stand the coffee they have in the breakroom."

Nathan stood. "This is my own. Black?"

"Yes, please."

He poured the last of the coffee into a disposable cup and handed it to her. "So, what do you have for me?"

She took a sip of the coffee, then sat it on his desk. "Thanks. I was at the site last night until midnight going through Elizabeth's car. Then, I came back here to log the evidence."

"Did you get any sleep?" he asked.

"I got a few hours in." She took another drink of the coffee.

"It sounds like you found something."

"Yes, and no. I found a rubber mallet in the trunk. It could have been what was used to hit Elizabeth on the head. I also found more candy wrappers."

"Candy wrappers?" Denzinger asked.

"Remember we found candy wrappers at Ann Parker's scene at the cemetery?" Nathan asked.

"Vaguely," he replied.

"The same wrappers were found in Isabella Osborne's car. I've seen the same candy at the Parker home, and at the bar where her first boyfriend works."

"I take it no DNA has been found on them?" Denzinger asked.

"None," Mallory said. "And, we won't find any on the ones from Elizabeth's car either. The salt water from the bay where the car was submerged would have deteriorated any that was there."

"I'd send the wrappers in for analysis anyway. You never know," Denzinger said.

"I have both the mallet and the wrappers ready to send to the state lab today."

"Did you find anything else?" Nathan asked.

"There were no fingerprints. The only other things found probably belonged to Elizabeth, except for one thing."

"What's that?"

"I found a brown cotton glove, also inside the trunk. There's no way to get a fingerprint from a cotton glove, and probably no DNA, since it was also soaked in the salt water, but I'm sending it to the lab too."

"What about traffic or security cameras?" Denzinger asked.

"Hank was the first officer on scene, and he stayed with

me until I left at midnight. I doubt he was able to check for any cameras, but Sergeant Donnelly should have his report. Hank's not due back on duty until this afternoon," Mallory said.

"I'll check with Donnelly," Nathan said. His intercom buzzed. "Yes?"

"Isabella Osborne is here to pick up her car," Gloria said.

Nathan looked at Mallory. "Can we release it?"

"Yes. I called her to come pick it up."

"Mallory will be up there in a few minutes with the paperwork for her to sign," he said.

Mallory stood, picking up her coffee. "I know you want to solve this, but I could sure use an easy day today." She winked at him before going out the door.

"I'll do what I can," he called after her.

"Promises, promises," she called out as she went to the hallway.

"You seem to have a lot of fun around here," Denzinger said.

"We manage to solve a few crimes too," Nathan answered.

"How's the PI working out?"

"It didn't. I kicked her out of the building yesterday. Well, technically the chief said to kick her out, but I got to do it."

"What'd she do?"

"It's a long story, but we think she was feeding William Parker information on the case. She was working for him, and I think her loyalties remained with him."

"I asked around about her work. She was very highly respected when she worked for Boston PD."

"Do you know why she left their department?" Nathan asked.

"No, but I'm guessing she got a better offer."

Sergeant Donnelly stepped into Nathan's office. "Sorry to interrupt. Oh, hello, Detective Denzinger."

"Donnelly."

"Nathan, we just found Ann Parker's car," Donnelly said.

"You just know Mallory is going to love hearing that," Denzinger said.

"I already told her. She wasn't amused, but she's on her way to the scene. I thought she was going to throw her coffee on me."

Nathan snickered. "Where was the car found?"

"Pay-to-park lot downtown."

"You mean her car has been in a parking lot this long, and it's just now been found?" Denzinger asked.

"We aren't sure how long it's been there. Officer Avery is checking on that as we speak," Donnelly said. He turned to leave.

"Shane," Nathan called to him. Donnelly stopped and came back into the office. "Could you email me Hank McCoy's report about Elizabeth Howe's car, if you have it?"

"Sure. I haven't read it yet, but as soon as I do, I'll send it over." Donnelly left.

"I think I'll head down to the lot," Nathan said. He looked at Denzinger. "Want to come along?"

"I'm at your disposal for the day."

When they arrived at the parking lot, Nathan saw that Mallory was already working on the car. He then spotted Officer Avery talking to the parking attendant. Avery walked over when Nathan and Denzinger got out of the car.

"Morning, Ryan. What have you found out?" Nathan asked.

"I drove through the lot early this morning checking license plates, and when I checked the plate against our stolen vehicle list, it was on there. I talked to the attendant, but he's not sure how long it's been here."

"He's not sure? Hey you, come over here!" Nathan shouted to the attendant.

The man slowly ambled over, not standing too close.

"What's your name?"

"John Wilson."

"How long has that car been there?" Nathan asked, pointing to the car.

"I-ah-I don't know, sir." He acted nervous, shifting his feet, as well as slowly moving away from the men.

"What the hell do you mean, you don't know? Was that car here when you left at the end of the day yesterday?" Nathan took a step closer to the attendant.

"There's a lot of cars still here when I leave every day. Tourists still shopping, people having dinner somewhere. It's a busy time of the year."

"What about in the mornings? Denzinger asked. "What do you do with the cars still here in the morning?"

"Well, they're supposed to be towed," he said.

"So, is this the first morning that car's been here?"

"I'm not sure."

Denzinger took a step closer to the man, who in sync took a step away. Denzinger took another step, as did the attendant again. Officer Avery stepped behind the man. One more step, and the man bumped into Avery.

"Where are you going?" Denzinger asked.

"He smells like marijuana," Avery said, not letting the attendant move any farther away.

Denzinger moved closer. "Are you high right now, Mr. Wilson?"

"What if I am? Pot's legal in this state now," he argued back.

"Did you drive to work this morning?" Nathan asked.

Wilson swallowed hard. "Yes."

"Put him in your car, Ryan. Then, call for a unit to take him to jail. Make sure they call the parking lot owner."

Avery took out his handcuffs.

"Wait a minute," Wilson protested. "I just said it's legal now."

"You just admitted driving to work high. Take him away," Nathan said.

Officer Avery handcuffed Wilson, then took him by the

arm to the police car.

"That's a bit of a problem," Denzinger said. "That guy's probably high every day he's at work."

"Yeah, he's useless. Hopefully, Mallory will be able to figure out how long the car's been here."

They walked over to the car where Mallory was searching the inside. The tow truck arrived and was backing up to the car.

"Busy morning, eh?" Nathan asked.

"I really don't want to hear your jokes," Mallory said.

"Well, maybe that grant will come through and you can hire an assistant."

"We can only hope." She got out of the car and waved to the tow truck driver to hook it up.

"Can you tell us anything?" Nathan asked.

"The doors were locked. It hadn't been hot-wired. I found the keys on top of the visor. It's hard to tell if it's been here since her murder. We've had both wet and dry weather since then, so the condition of the car likely won't be an indicator."

Nathan looked around the lot. "I don't see any security cameras on the lot. Are there any traffic cams in the area?"

"Avery said there are no traffic cameras, but some of the businesses might have security cameras," she said.

"I'll have him canvas the businesses, once the other unit comes to take the attendant in for booking."

"What?"

Nathan looked at Mallory. "He's high."

"Great," Mallory said. "I did find this." She handed Nathan a clear evidence bag. "It's an envelope addressed to Ann with no return address. I want to wait until we get back to the PD to open it."

The tow truck motor revved up. "Stand back, please," the operator shouted. They did as he instructed.

"I want to know what's in that envelope as soon as you open it," Nathan said loudly over the truck motor.

"Will do, Boss," Mallory said.

Nathan and Denzinger started back to the car as Avery approached.

"Wilson is on his way into the PD, and I called the owner of the lot."

"Thanks, Ryan. I have one more job for you. After Mallory leaves with the vehicle, can you check with the businesses on the street to see if they have any security cameras that might have caught someone leaving the car here?"

"Yes, sir. What timeline should I look for?"

"The murder took place on the night of September twenty-third. If any of them have cameras, they probably won't loop that far back, so whatever you can find will be fine. I'll have another officer come down to help with the canvassing."

"Yes, sir." Avery headed over to Mallory, while Nathan and Denzinger continued to their car.

When they reached the car, Nathan stopped. "Do you see that?" He stared across the street.

"What am I looking at?" Denzinger asked.

Nathan didn't answer. Instead, he walked across the street. Denzinger followed. Nathan came to a stop in front of a business. "This is Joe Cassidy's office."

"His office is directly across from the parking lot," Denzinger pointed out.

"Nathan! Nathan Perry. I need to talk to you," Cassidy shouted, stepping out of his office.

"What do you want, Joe?"

"Come in here. I don't want to talk out here." He motioned his hand for Nathan to come inside.

"Your suspect is inviting you in to talk," Denzinger mumbled to Nathan. "It doesn't get much easier than that."

"I know. That's what bothers me."

Nathan and Denzinger walked into Joe's building. Once inside, Joe turned to the men. "Nathan, I'm in trouble," Joe said, then looked past Nathan at Denzinger. "I don't want to talk in front of him."

"If you're going to talk to me, you'll have to do it in front of Detective Denzinger too. Now, how are you in trouble?"

Joe looked at his secretary at her desk, and then back at Nathan. "Let's go to my office."

Both officers followed Cassidy down the hall to his office, and sat down.

"Tell me about your trouble," Nathan said.

"I got a call from a detective in Salem." He waved his hands around while speaking. "He wants to talk to me about the witch that was burned there. What do I do?"

"You talk to him, Joe."

"What if he thinks I did it?"

"Did you do it?" Denzinger asked.

"No," he said, rather matter-of-factly.

"Then, you have nothing to worry about," Nathan said. "If you're that worried about it, take an attorney with you. There's plenty to choose from here in Mystic. You must have worked for at least a few of them."

Joe lowered his head. "None of the lawyers here like me. They think I'm a fool."

Nathan looked at Denzinger, who was shaking his head. "Joe, look at me. Call an attorney in Salem."

"I can do that, but why do they think I did it?"

"You don't know that's what they think," Nathan said.

"Did you know the victim?" Denzinger asked.

He didn't answer.

"Joe," Nathan said. "Did you know the woman from Salem?"

"I did. We actually went out for coffee a couple times." He buried his head in his hands.

"You said you didn't do it. Did you ever think you might have some information about her that could help with the investigation?"

Joe looked up. "But they think I did it."

"Talk to them. Convince them otherwise."

Joe nodded his head. "I will. I will."

Nathan and Denzinger stood to leave. Before going out the door, Nathan turned back to Joe. "Just make sure you have a lawyer with you."

Back out on the street, the men reached Nathan's car. "I think you have a new prime suspect," Denzinger said.

"Yeah. He's at least moved up to number two on my list."

After stopping for lunch, the two officers returned to the police department. "I want to check with Mallory to see if she found anything in Ann Parker's car yet," Nathan said.

They went to her office, but found it locked up tight.

"Maybe she's at lunch," Denzinger suggested.

"We can check up front." They walked to the front desk. "Gloria, is Mallory at lunch? Her office is locked," Nathan said.

"She's still out in the garage going through the car that was brought in this morning."

"Thanks." They walked across the rear parking lot to the garage. The big door was closed, so they entered through the smaller door. It opened into a room with a counter and a desk. An older officer behind the counter looked up when they came in. Mallory sat at the desk, typing on a computer.

"We're here to see her," Nathan said, nodding toward Mallory.

She looked up. "I wondered when you'd be here."

Nathan and Denzinger walked around the counter to her desk. "We went to lunch," Nathan said.

"That's nice. I haven't slept, had breakfast, or lunch yet."

Denzinger took a step back, leaving Nathan in the line of fire.

"I'll have some food delivered for you." He took out his phone.

"Thanks, but you don't have to. I'm almost finished, and then I'm going home to sleep. Salem CSU said they would cover for me in case something comes up."

Nathan put his phone back in his pocket. "Did you find anything in Ann's car?"

"No fingerprints or candy wrappers. Here's that envelope

and letter you wanted to see. I'll send it to the state lab so they can work their magic on it. Maybe they can find something." She handed him a clear evidence bag.

Nathan took the letter. Denzinger stood next to him as they read it. "This is from her uncle, the priest, pleading for her to come home and make up with her parents."

"He tells her that her father hasn't been the same since she left," Denzinger added. "I wonder how he was different."

"I think we need to speak with Father Mike," Nathan said. He handed the evidence bag back to Mallory. He and Denzinger started to leave.

"Don't you want to know what else I found?" Mallory asked.

Both men stopped and turned. "You found something else?"

"I didn't find her amulet, but I did find some rosary beads." She held up another evidence bag with a set of beads inside.

Nathan took the bag. "We need to find out if these are Ann's. Did you find anything else?"

Mallory was in mid-yawn when he asked. "No, but I never got a chance to talk to you about Mac Dupont's devices."

He gave the evidence bag back to her. "What did you find?"

"It didn't look like she emailed any records to anyone. That doesn't mean she didn't copy something onto a flash drive, for either herself, or someone else, though."

"Thanks, Mallory. I guess you can mail her stuff to her office."

"That's going to be expensive. You don't want her to pick them up?" she asked.

"I don't want her back in the building, and I'm pretty sure the chief doesn't either."

"Gotcha."

He and Denzinger headed across the parking lot back to the police department. Nathan did his best to hide his limp, but his leg was hurting more than usual this afternoon.

They were almost back to the building when Denzinger spoke up. "Are you limping?"

Nathan stopped and leaned against one of the police cars. "Yes, it's my leg, from the injury I received in Afghanistan. I've been having a lot of pain recently."

"I can see that. Have you had it checked?"

"Not yet. I have to go to Walter Reed in D.C. for that. I can't leave in the middle of an investigation. I'll go as soon as an arrest is made. Please don't mention this to anyone. I'd like to keep this between us for now."

"You have my word."

They continued walking to the building, and into Nathan's office. He sat down at his desk, took a bottle of aspirin out of the drawer, and took two. Denzinger sat across the desk from him.

"I want to see if Ann Parker's uncle will talk to us about her. Want to stick around?" he asked Denzinger.

"I told you I was here for the day," Denzinger replied.

Nathan found Father Mike's phone number in the case file. He pushed the speaker button on the phone and dialed.

After two rings, the call was answered. "Hello."

"Is this Father Michael Dunbar?" Nathan asked.

"It is."

"This is Detective Perry from the Mystic Police Department."

"Hello, Detective. What can I do for you?"

"Would it be possible for you to come to Mystic to meet with me?"

"Am I a suspect now?" the priest asked.

Nathan looked at Denzinger. "No. We found Ann's car, and in it we found a letter from you. We thought you could tell us about her frame of mind. It read as though you'd been in contact with her."

"I only had contact with her via the mail. What time do you want me there?"

"Could you be at the police department by three o'clock?"

"I think I can manage that," Father Mike said.

"Good. I'll see you then." Nathan ended the call.

By three-o'clock that afternoon, Father Mike had arrived. He was waiting in the interrogation room when Gloria stopped Nathan and Denzinger as they were walking to the room.

"You should know something before you go in," she said.

"What?"

"He brought someone with him, and you're not going to like it."

"An attorney? I'd be shocked if he didn't bring one," Nathan said.

"It's not an attorney. Mac Dupont came with him."

Nathan could feel his face burning, but didn't say anything.

Denzinger made a suggestion. "Why don't you let me question him? You can watch from the observation room. I'm familiar enough with the case, and Dupont could be a distraction to you."

Nathan thought for a few seconds. "That's probably a good idea." He handed Denzinger the case file. "Gloria, accompany the detective in the interview. I want someone from this department represented in there."

"Of course," she replied.

Nathan went to the observation room. When Denzinger and Gloria walked into the interrogation room, Mac looked surprised.

"Good afternoon," Denzinger began. "I'm Detective Denzinger from the state police and this is Officer Wheeler from the Mystic PD."

"Where's Nathan?" Mac asked.

"He had another commitment and asked if I could handle this interview."

Gloria spoke up. "Why are you here, Miss Dupont?"

"Father Mike called me. He asked me to drive him down

here," she replied.

"I wanted someone to be with me; as a witness, if I needed one," the priest said.

As Nathan watched, Mac looked at the mirrored window in the room, as if she knew he was standing there.

"Thank you for coming in, Father," Denzinger said. "The first thing I want to ask is if you've ever seen this before?" He put the evidence bag on the table that held the rosary beads found in Ann's car.

Father Mike picked up the bag and looked closely at it. Nathan noticed his hand was shaking. Suddenly, the priest's eyes widened and he dropped the bag back on the table. "Those are Ann's rosary beads. Where did you find them?" He appeared shaken.

"You're sure they're hers?" Denzinger asked.

"Yes. I'm sure. I gave them to her when she graduated from high school."

"Where did you get them?" Mac asked.

"They were found under the seat of her car."

Denzinger continued with the questioning. "As Detective Perry said on the phone with you, we found Ann's car, and in it was a letter you had written to her. How long had you been in contact with her?"

"I wrote to her about a month before she was killed. Her father was becoming more and more depressed by her absence. He had found out her address here in Mystic, and I saw it on a notepad on his desk. I decided to write to her, to try to mediate a reconciliation between them. She wrote back declining my request."

"Do you have her letter?"

"No, I'm afraid I don't. William didn't know that I had written to her and I didn't want him finding it. I destroyed it."

"What did she say in her reply to you?" Gloria asked.

"She said she was happy, and wasn't interested in continuing a relationship with her family."

"How many times did you and Ann correspond?"

"I sent her two letters, but she only replied after the first one."

"In the letter we found, it sounded like you were also trying to get her to return to church. Why would you ask her about that?" Denzinger asked.

"The church is my domicile, my work, even though I'm retired. William told me that she was working in a store that sold demonic items. I didn't think that was a proper place for her to work."

"Mr. Parker knew she was working at the witch store?" Gloria asked.

"Yes."

"What did her parents think about that?"

"I don't think William ever told Margaret where she worked. He wasn't happy about Ann's employment there at all."

"How so?" Gloria asked.

"Well, he didn't think it was a proper place either."

"Father, you said you didn't want Mr. Parker to know that you knew Ann's address, but if you knew her address, and you knew how he felt about where she worked, you must have discussed it with him," Denzinger said.

"William told me she was in Mystic and where she worked, just not her address. I think he needed someone to talk to about her since he hadn't told Margaret yet."

"Yet?" Gloria asked.

Mac jumped in. "Mr. Parker didn't tell his wife how much he knew until after Ann's death. He said it was the hardest thing he ever had to do, and regrets keeping it from her."

Denzinger looked at Mac. "If Father Mike found out Ann's address, what's the chance Mrs. Parker found the address the same way?"

"I suppose its possible, but not likely," she replied.

"Why not?"

Mac paused before answering. "She rarely went into his study. That was his domain."

"Wait a minute. Do you think Margaret did this to Ann? That's preposterous," Father Mike said.

"I'm covering all possibilities," Denzinger said.

Father Mike had reached his breaking point. He stood up, leaning over the table toward Denzinger. "My sister is a saint! She would never hurt her daughter. She loved Ann more than anything."

"What about Mr. Parker?" Denzinger asked.

This time, Mac stood. "I think we're done." She took Father Mike by the arm, and led him out. Before walking out of the room, she looked at Denzinger. "Tell Nathan I knew he didn't have the balls to finish this." She then looked at the two-way mirror before walking out.

Watching from the observation room, Nathan was furious, no doubt what Mac wanted. He wanted to open the door to confront her in the hallway, but held back. He didn't want to give her the satisfaction of getting under his skin.

After a few minutes, the door opened, and Denzinger stepped in. "I thought for sure you'd be waiting for Dupont in the hall," Denzinger said.

"That's just what she wanted. I assume they've left?"

"Gloria walked them to the lobby to make sure Mac didn't take a turn into your office."

They walked to Nathan office.

"Have you changed your thoughts about William Parker as your prime suspect?"

"Not really."

Gloria approached as they reached Nathan's office. "Daniel Grant left some information for you while we were in the interview." She handed him a file folder.

They went into his office. Nathan sat down behind his desk to look through the file. Denzinger sat in front of the desk, and Gloria stood in the doorway.

"This is the Child Services report. Mrs. Parker was the perpetrator in the report, not Mr. Parker." He continued reading. "There were small incidents of abuse, but nothing severe. She signed an agreement for counseling, and if no more evidence of abuse was found in the following twelve months, the report would be purged. Get this, she was prescribed Valium."

"Valium?" Denzinger asked.

"Valium was found in both Ann Parker and Elizabeth Howe's toxicology report," Nathan said. "I wonder if she still takes it."

"If so, Parker could have gotten the drug from his wife's bottle."

"That's a possibility."

"Apparently, there was more abuse, if you have the report. Is there anything else in there?" Denzinger asked.

Nathan quickly looked through the file. "I don't see any other reports."

"Mr. Grant said the department got way behind in their file purging. That's why the file was still there," Gloria said.

Nathan closed the file and put it on his desk. "I can't imagine frail little Margaret Parker being able to hang Ann's body from a tree. I'm sticking with William as my prime suspect."

Chapter Thirteen

The next morning, Nathan had just started a pot of coffee in his office when Detective Denzinger walked in.

"What are you doing here?" Nathan asked.

"I had so much fun yesterday, I couldn't stay away."

"Have a seat. The coffee should be done in a few minutes."

"How's your leg this morning?" Denzinger sat down.

"Not too bad, but it's early." Nathan put the aspirin bottle from the top of his desk into the drawer. "Have you had breakfast?"

"A sausage and egg biscuit from a drive-thru. You?"

"Biscuits and gravy from the café."

"We're sure healthy eaters, aren't we?"

Nathan laughed as he got up to pour the coffee. When he handed Denzinger a cup, Mallory walked in holding a file folder, and an empty cup.

"I'll trade you what I have in this folder for what you have in that pot," she said.

"Let's make a deal." He poured coffee into her cup. "Did you get any sleep?"

Mallory sat next to Denzinger in front of Nathan's desk, taking a sip of coffee before answering. "Thanks. Not as much as I would have liked."

"What do you have for me?" He sat back behind his desk.

"Thanks to Detective Denzinger, I received the forensic report this morning from both Ann Parker and Elizabeth Howe's cars."

"You're welcome." Denzinger raised his coffee cup. Mallory did the same, clinking cups with him.

"Unfortunately, there was no DNA found. Any fingerprints found were not clear enough to get even a partial match."

"You said it was a long shot." Nathan took a drink of coffee.

"However, we did get a break. Officer Avery found security camera footage of the parking lot where Ann's car was found. It showed the car being left there three days ago."

"Could the driver be identified?" Denzinger asked.

"All you can see is that it's an older man."

"William Parker?" Nathan asked.

"The video wasn't clear enough for an I.D. I tried to clean it up, but it didn't help," she said. "We might have caught a break, though. The footage showed a car picking the man up."

"Was the license number visible?"

"The angle wasn't right. There was no way to read it."

"Anything else?"

"No, that's it. I'll email you a copy of the video as soon as I get back to my office." Mallory picked up her coffee from the desk and left.

"At least we have the video," Denzinger said.

Nathan's desk phone buzzed. He pushed the speaker button. "Yes?"

"Joe Cassidy is here. He insists on seeing you," Gloria said.

Nathan let out a deep breath. "Send him back."

Before Nathan could get to the door, Joe Cassidy stood in the doorway with an officer behind him.

"Nathan, I really need to talk to you," Joe said.

"Thank you, Officer Davis. Come in, Joe."

He took one step into the office. "I need to talk to you, but not with him around." He nodded toward Denzinger.

"I'll wait in the break room," Denzinger said, standing up.

"No, stay here. I'll take him to another office."

"Can I use your computer while you're gone? I need to check in with work."

"Sure."

Nathan walked down the hallway with Joe on his heels. At the end of the hall, Nathan stopped. "We can talk in here."

Joe followed him into the office and sat down. "This is that lady PI's office you worked with on the case. Where is she?"

Nathan sat down. "She went back to Boston. What do you want to see me about?"

"Did the detective from Salem call you?"

"No, why would he?"

"After you and I talked yesterday morning, I went to Salem to talk to them, just like you said I should. I told them I didn't kill Marilyn. That's the lady that died there."

"You still haven't said why you're here."

"I-I don't think they believed me. I thought maybe they called you." Joe slumped back in the chair. "Could I have some water? I'm really thirsty."

Nathan noticed Joe was having trouble breathing. "Are you okay?"

"I feel like I'm going to be sick."

Nathan walked out into the hallway. "Sergeant Donnelly, I have a situation in here. Could you bring some water, and call an ambulance?"

"What's wrong?" Donnelly asked.

"Joe Cassidy is about to fall out on me."

Donnelly stepped into the nearest office. A short time later, she came back with a bottle of water. By that time, Joe was on the floor, doubled over with stomach pain. Nathan kneeled over him. Donnelly opened the water bottle and handed it to Nathan. "Joe, can you sit up to drink some water?"

He sat up as best he could. Nathan helped him with the bottle as he drank a few sips. "Thanks," Joe said. He had to lay back down.

"The ambulance will be here soon to take you to the hospital. They'll find out what's wrong," Nathan assured him.

"I know what's wrong. I ate breakfast this morning, and then forgot to take my insulin. My blood sugar is probably too high."

"You're diabetic?"

The paramedics arrived before Joe could answer. Nathan moved away to let them attend to Joe. "He said he needs insulin."

Denzinger stood in the hallway, as well as several other officers. Nathan nodded to him to follow. He stopped at the end of the hallway.

"What happened?" Denzinger asked.

"His blood sugar spiked."

"He's diabetic?"

"That's what I said when he told me. If he's diabetic, he couldn't be the killer. All that candy would have put him into a diabetic coma," Nathan said.

The paramedics wheeled Joe down the hallway on the stretcher. They had started an IV, and he had an oxygen mask over his nose and mouth.

"Thanks, Nathan," he said as they passed.

"I'll check on you later, Joe." Nathan and Denzinger went into Nathan's office and sat down. Gloria and Hank walked in behind them.

"What happened?" Gloria asked.

"I think Joe was on the verge of a diabetic coma," Nathan said.

"Joe's diabetic?" Hank asked.

"It's like an echo," Nathan said. "Apparently, he is. I didn't know either."

"Those candy wrappers in evidence couldn't be his then," Gloria said.

"Exactly. I think we can rule him out as a suspect now."

"Wait a minute," Denzinger said. "Sometimes, diabetics need sugar, like when their sugar level is too low, right?"

"If he'd eaten that much candy, he would've been dead at the scene," Gloria pointed out.

"You're probably right," Denzinger conceded.

"Is William Parker still the main suspect then?" Hank asked, walking up to them.

"It's good to see you back on day shift, Hank. Yes, I'm still leaning toward Mr. Parker."

"This is beginning to sound like a rerun. I'm going back to the front desk," Gloria said.

"I was about to leave on patrol. Call me, if you need anything." Hank left also.

"I heard an email come in while you were with Cassidy. Maybe it was the video from your tech." Denzinger got up to pour himself another cup of coffee. "What did Cassidy want to talk to you about?"

"He was still worried about being a suspect in the Salem murder." Nathan started typing on his computer. "Here it is."

Denzinger walked around the desk to look at the monitor. Nathan started the video. "The time stamp shows seven a.m."

"Just after sunrise," Denzinger said. "There's Miss Parker's car turning into the parking lot."

"Damn it. He parked it right in the glare of the sun."

"There he goes across the lot."

"He's walking kind of slow," Nathan pointed out.

"If it's William Parker, it's not too slow. He's an old man." Denzinger took a drink of coffee.

"There's the car picking him up." Nathan jotted down the description of the car, then his phone buzzed. "What do you need, Gloria?"

"Levi Sabin from Animal Control is on line one. He needs some assistance on a call."

Nathan looked at Denzinger, shaking his head. "I really don't have time. Would you have a patrol unit dispatched to assist him?"

"I already tried, but he specifically asked for you."

"Okay, I'll talk to him." Nathan pushed line one, leaving the speaker on. "Levi, Nathan Perry. What can I do for you?"

"I hate to bother you, but I don't have any arrest powers. I can only write citations. I think you'll be interested in this. When we first met, you asked about mutilated animals. Just now, I received a report about someone mutilating cats at a home on Summer Street."

Nathan looked at Denzinger. "You're right. I'm interested."

"The call came in fifteen minutes ago, so we need to go. I'm the only one on duty, unarmed, and I really don't want to go alone," Sabin said.

"Meet me on Bridge Street. We're leaving right now." Nathan hung up the call. "Want to go?" he asked Denzinger.

"I do."

Denzinger rushed out the back door of the building, Nathan followed, not as quickly. With lights and siren on, they left the parking lot. Nathan picked up the microphone. "Dispatch, six-nineteen. Detective Denzinger and I are enroute to assist Animal Control on a call on Summer Street. Have five-thirteen meet me on Bridge Street to also assist."

"Roger, six-nineteen," the dispatcher replied.

Nathan replaced the mic. "After I saw on the crime scene report that there was cat blood on Ann Parker's clothes, I contacted Animal Control about any mutilation reports."

"That was good thinking," Denzinger said.

Nathan turned on Bridge Street. "There's Levi." He turned off the lights and siren, pulling the car next to the Animal Control truck.

"That was fast," Levi said.

"You said we needed to go. This is Detective Denzinger from the state police. He was in my office when you called, and decided to tag along."

"Nice to meet you, sir."

"You, too," Denzinger said.

Hank pulled up next to Nathan's car. "What's up?"

Levi needs our help and it may be connected to the witch murders," Nathan said.

"The guy was at the dump earlier, but he's home now," Levi said. "His house is down on the next street. His name is Phillip Reilly. He's nineteen, unemployed, and still lives with his mother. I've received reports from their neighbors that he's been killing animals in the backyard and enjoying the mutilations a little too much."

"Let's go get him," Nathan said.

"Wait," Sabin said. "I think his mother is home. Can we not go in guns a blazin'?"

Nathan heard Denzinger trying to hold back a laugh. "We don't do it that way. We'll follow you to the house."

Sabin drove off with Nathan falling in behind him, and Hank bringing up the rear.

"I think that guy has seen too many cop shows," Denzinger joked.

"He's nervous. The most exciting thing he's probably done is pick up stray dogs. I'll keep an eye on him."

Sabin stopped his truck in front of a house on Summer Street. All of the officers grouped on the sidewalk.

"We don't know what this kid is into, and since his mother may be in the house, let's take it easy to start," Nathan said. "Levi and I will knock on the front door. Sam, you and Hank cover the rear of the house in case he runs."

With their assignments made, the officers headed to their areas. Before knocking, Nathan turned to Sabin, "Stay behind me. Don't say anything to Reilly to anger him. In fact, I should probably do most of the talking, if you're okay with that?"

A relieved look went over Sabin's face. "I'm more than okay with that."

With that being said, Nathan knocked on the door. It took several knocks before a woman answered the door. "Can I help you?"

"Good morning. I'm Nathan Perry with the Mystic Police Department." He held up his badge. "This is Levi Sabin with Animal Control. We're looking for Phillip Reilly."

"I'm his mother. What did he do this time?"

Not the response he was hoping for from his mother. "Probably nothing, ma'am. Is he here? We really need to speak with him."

"He's in the garage." She motioned to the right of the house.

"Is he by himself?"

"As far as I know."

"Thank you. Please go back in the house," Nathan said. He and Sabin started toward the garage.

"Wait a minute. What did he do?" Reilly's mother shouted.

Without warning, the side door of the garage flew open, and a man ran out, heading down the street.

"That's him," Sabin shouted.

Nathan started after him. "Go get Sam and Hank," he yelled back at Sabin.

Reilly had a good lead when he ran between two buildings. Nathan followed him into the dead-end alley. Reilly was trying to get over the fence, but was failing.

"Police! Get your ass back here!" Nathan shouted between gasps for air, his leg throbbing.

Reilly turned, and started walking toward Nathan, who was reaching for his handcuffs. Suddenly, he tried to sprint passed Nathan, who tackled him like a linebacker hitting a quarterback. A scuffle ensued with Nathan rolling Reilly onto his stomach and handcuffing him, just as Sam, Hank, and Levi found them.

"Thanks for showing up," Nathan said, still out of breath. He slid off of Reilly so Hank could take control of him. Something was wrong, Nathan thought, laying on the pavement. He had a burning sensation throbbing through his knee, radiating up into his thigh. "Levi, go with Hank to take

Reilly to the car."

Hank pulled Reilly up to a standing position. He and Sabin walked him out of the alley.

"This was not a good day to be running," Nathan said, trying to sit up.

Sam held out his hand to pull him up. As soon as Nathan put weight on his left leg, he let out a groan and went back down, holding his knee. "Damn it. I don't think I can walk."

"Hang on." Sam ran out to the street. "Hank, call an ambulance. Nathan's hurt.

A few minutes later, Hank and Levi pulled their vehicles up to the alley where Nathan and Hank waited. Reilly sat in the backseat of Hank's car, staring toward Nathan on the ground.

"The ambulance is on the way. What happened?" Hank asked.

"Bad tackle, I guess," he replied.

"You always were better on offense, than defense," Hank said.

A few minutes later, the ambulance pulled to a stop on the street, along with what looked like every police car in Mystic.

"What did you tell them when you called in?" Nathan asked Hank.

"I radioed dispatch and told them I needed an ambulance because you were hurt. You know everyone is going to show up when an officer is down."

Nathan smiled. "You're right. Thanks."

The paramedics walked up to check Nathan. They took his vitals, and checked for broken bones. Then, with the help of a couple other officers, they helped Nathan onto the stretcher they had wheeled down.

"Thanks, everyone. I'm sure I'll be fine," Nathan said to all the officers as he was wheeled to the ambulance.

Hank had another officer take Reilly in, so he could follow the ambulance to the hospital.

After many hours in the emergency room, they finally released Nathan. He was brought into the waiting area in a wheelchair. A brace was strapped to his left leg from below his knee to mid-thigh. He was greeted by Hank, Levi, and Dana.

"What are you doing here?" Nathan asked her.

"Hank called me. I came right over."

"You didn't have to."

"Yes, I did," she said. "You'd do the same thing for me."

A smile spread across his face. "I would."

"What did the doctor say was wrong with your leg?" Hank asked.

"I have a subluxation of the left knee."

"What does that mean?" Levi asked.

"In jock terms, I blew out my knee. It's my old injury from Afghanistan coming back to haunt me. Can one you take me to the police department?"

"Wait a minute," Dana protested. "You're not going back to work. I'll take you home."

"No. I need to get back to work. I have a suspect to question."

Dana scowled at him. "You are one stubborn man. I'll wait for you at your house." She started to leave.

"Dana, wait." He took his keys out of his pocket, taking one off the ring, and handing it to her. "You'll need this."

She took the key, holding his hand a little longer than normal. "I'm holding you boys responsible to make sure he gets home in one piece," she demanded.

"I'll watch him," Hank said.

Dana let go of Nathan's hand, leaving.

"Can you bend your knee to get in the car?" Hank asked.

"I can. Where's the crutches they gave me?"

"Right here, Mr. Perry," the nurse said.

Levi took the crutches from her. Nathan pushed the wheelchair out to the police car, followed by Levi.

"Where's my gun and badge?" Nathan asked.

"I locked them in my trunk."

"How long will you be laid up?" Levi asked.

"Longer than I want. It's probably going to take surgery to fix this."

When they reached the car, Hank opened the door. Nathan locked the wheels on his chair. Levi held the chair while Nathan slowly stood up, and eventually slid into the passenger seat of the car.

"Levi, meet us at the police department. I'm going to question Reilly," Nathan said.

"Will do." Levi handed Hank the crutches, then took the wheelchair back inside.

Before Hank got into the car, he got Nathan's badge and gun from the trunk. Before long, they were on the road, headed to the police department.

"Where's Denzinger?" Nathan asked.

"He should be in your office. He wanted to be available to question Reilly, in case you couldn't."

"Good. You better let me out in front of the building. I don't think I can navigate the steps in the back."

"No problem. I had Ryan Avery drive your personal vehicle home from the PD. I didn't think you'd be able to do that."

"Thanks."

Hank pulled up in front of the police department. He got out and rushed around the car before Nathan could get out. "You sure you can handle these crutches?"

"I'm an old pro at this." He got out of the car, relying heavily on the crutches to hold him up. "I was on them for a long time after Afghanistan."

Nathan walked into the lobby with Hank following. He saw Gloria at the front desk immediately hang up the phone. She met him at the doorway to the hall.

"What are you doing here? You should be at home," she said.

"I'm doing fine. Thanks for asking," he joked. "I have a case to solve." He started a slow walk down the hallway to his office. Hank and Gloria followed. Every officer along the way stopped to offer any help they could. Nathan was appreciative of their kindness.

When he reached his office, he saw Denzinger sitting at his desk. "Taking over, eh?"

"Nathan." Denzinger immediately got up to let Nathan sit down. "Hank texted saying you were coming in. What the hell were you thinking? You need to be home."

"I've heard that way too many times in the last hour."

"You're about to hear it again," Chief Cabot said, standing in the doorway.

Nathan knew he had to head this off. "Chief, we're so close to solving the case. I have to finish it."

The chief had a stern look on his face. No one in the room dared to speak. He stared at Nathan for what seemed like minutes before speaking again. "All right, but there are some conditions."

"I'll do whatever you say."

"I'm restricting you to desk duty only."

"Yes, sir."

"You have a week to find your killer, unless the doctors say different. Then you're on medical leave."

"A week?"

"That's right," the chief said. "Detective Denzinger has agreed to take over the investigation with the assistance of Officers McCoy and Wheeler. That's final. Keep me updated." Being all business, Chief Cabot left as quickly as he came.

Nathan looked at Denzinger. "Traitor."

Denzinger held up his hands in surrender. "Chief Cabot was hinting that I should take over since you were hurt. If I hadn't volunteered, he would have called my supervisor to request it."

Just then, Levi stepped into the office. "Sorry I'm late."

"You're right on time. Hank, would you have Reilly taken to Interrogation Room One?"

"Sure." Hank left the office.

Nathan stood. "I need to be sitting in the room when Reilly comes in. Levi, come with me."

"Really?"

"Yes. If it weren't for you, we wouldn't have a suspect in custody."

"If it weren't for me, you wouldn't be on crutches," Levi replied, in a quiet voice.

Nathan stopped. "Believe me, I eventually would have."

Levi looked confused.

"It's a long story."

When Hank brought Reilly into the interrogation room, Nathan and Levi were already sitting at the table. Reilly sat down opposite them. Hank connected Reilly's handcuffs to the metal bracket attached to the top of the table. He then stood next to the door. "He's waived his rights."

"Mr. Reilly, I'm Detective Perry and this is Levi Sabin with Animal Control. Do you know why you were arrested?"

"Because I couldn't get past you in the alley?"

"That would be the resisting arrest charge, but not what I'm talking about. Levi, tell him what he's charged with."

"My department received numerous complaints about you killing and then mutilating cats."

"Yeah, so what?"

"It's illegal, dumbass," Nathan said.

"It is? I didn't know that."

"Why would you do such a thing?" Levi asked.

"For the money?"

"What?" Nathan couldn't believe what he was hearing. "What money?"

"Some dude was paying me money to get him cat blood."

Nathan looked at Hank, who looked as surprised as Nathan felt. "Who is this--dude?"

"I don't know his name. He called me one day about a month ago asking if I could get him some cat blood. After I got him the first batch, he wanted a new batch every week. He paid good money."

"And, again, illegal," Levi said.

"What did the man look like?" Nathan asked.

"He was an older guy. I called him Preacher, like in that Clint Eastwood movie."

The hairs stood up on Nathan's neck. "Why Preacher?"

"Cause he wore the same kind of collar as Clint did in that movie."

"Did Preacher say why he needed the blood?"

"I asked him about that when I got him the first batch. He wouldn't answer, but I figured it out." Reilly was sounding cocky.

"Enlighten me."

"Huh?"

"Tell me what you figured out," Nathan simplified, shaking his head.

"I think he was really one of those devil worshipers."

"You didn't feel bad about helping a devil worshiper?" Levi asked.

"No, man. Like I said, Preacher paid me good."

There was a knock at the door, and Denzinger stepped into the room.

Looking through the file folder on the table, Nathan found what he needed. "Is this Preacher?" He showed Reilly a photo from the file.

"That's the guy!" Reilly said, pointing to the photo.

Nathan looked at Hank and Denzinger. "Father Mike. Hank, would you have an officer take Mr. Reilly back to his cell?"

Hank unlocked Reilly's handcuffs, and took him out of the room.

"I can't believe he identified Father Mike," Nathan said to Denzinger.

"Who's Father Mike?" Levi said.

"My new murder suspect."

"Wow. This is way above my pay grade. I probably should let you guys do your job." Levi got up to leave.

"I'll have an officer get in touch with you on Monday about filing charges on Reilly," Nathan said. "In the meantime, get your report written. I'll need a copy of it."

"Thanks for helping me, but sorry you ended up hurt," Levi said.

"No, thank you for helping me crack this murder case."

Levi smiled with pride. As he went out, Hank came back in. "What just happened in here?"

"I think Reilly just handed us our murderer," Nathan said.

"Why would Father Mike kill his own niece?" Denzinger said.

"We'll just have to ask him that when we arrest him."

"We?" Denzinger asked. "I believe I heard Chief Cabot restrict you to desk duty."

"If you think I'm going to miss this arrest, you're crazy. Let's go call Daniel Grant to get an arrest warrant."

Even though it was late on Friday, the District Attorney stayed to get the warrant processed. He delivered it to Nathan personally. "What happened to you?" he asked when he saw Nathan with the brace on his leg.

"I aggravated an old injury."

"Are you going to be okay?" He handed the warrant to Nathan.

"Yes. Thanks. We'll keep you updated."

"Good luck." The District Attorney left.

"Let's go get him." Nathan started to get up.

"Hold on," Denzinger said. "You've had a long day with everything that happened to you. You need to go home and rest. Father Mike has no idea we're on to him. He'll still be there tomorrow."

"I can manage," Nathan said, bracing himself on his desk, struggling to stand up.

"Isn't Dana waiting at your house? She'll cut your good leg off, and shoot me, if you don't show up soon," Hank said.

"And, I'll tell Chief Cabot, if you don't go home." Gloria walked into the office.

"Were you listening in the hallway?" Nathan asked.

"I was walking by on the way to my car, and I'm not kidding. If you don't go home, I'll tell the chief."

"Another traitor," he replied with a smile. "Okay. Hank, take me home. We'll meet back here in the morning at eight."

"Let's make that nine. You aren't moving as fast as usual," Denzinger said.

Dana was waiting at the door when Hank pulled into Nathan's driveway. Both she and Hank helped him onto the porch and into the house. "I was getting worried."

Nathan went into the living room, and sat on the couch, putting his leg up on the coffee table. "Thanks, Hank."

"I'll pick you up around eight-thirty in the morning," Hank said, going out the door.

"What are you doing at eight-thirty?" Dana asked.

"The arrest we made today has led us to the person who we think murdered the two women and assaulted Isabella Osborne. We're going to arrest the suspect tomorrow. Oh, that's off the record for now. Could you bring me some water?"

Dana brought him a glass of water. He took a prescription bottle out of his shirt pocket, and took two pills.

She took the bottle from him and looked at it. "You're in pain. You're in no condition to go arrest anyone. There are plenty of officers at the police department that can do it."

"Hank and Sam will be with me, and I'll probably take another officer or two."

Dana could only shake her head. "I asked Ginger to bring something here for dinner. I ate mine and put yours in the oven. Are you hungry?"

"Actually, I am. I haven't eaten all day."

He started to get up, but Dana stopped him. Instead of eating in the kitchen, she brought his food on a tray to the couch. He ate there, while telling her what happened with the arrest, still off the record, he reminded her.

"Are you spending the night here?" he asked.

"Yes. I stopped by my place and packed a bag."

"Where are you sleeping?"

"In your bed."

"Good." He smiled, then yawned.

"Seriously? You can barely walk, and you're thinking about sex?"

"I can't help it." He yawned again.

"After those pain killers take effect, you'll be asleep before you hit the pillow," she said.

"You're probably right. I think I need to head to bed now."

Dana followed him down the hall to the bedroom. She was right. He was asleep not long after he laid down

Saturday morning, Nathan, Denzinger, Hank, Gloria, Sergeant Donnelly, Officer Avery, and Mallory arrived at the Parker house in Foxborough to arrest Father Mike and search his residence.

"Denzinger and I will go in and make the arrest," Nathan said. "Hank, you and Gloria should probably come with me. Sergeant Donnelly and Officer Avery, stand by, paying particular attention to see if anyone leaves the property. Father Mike is an older gentleman. I don't think we'll have any trouble, but you just never know."

"What about me?" Mallory asked.

"Father Mike lives in the pool house around back. We have a warrant to search the premises. Once he's in custody, you can come with us to do the search."

The officers went to the front door and rang the doorbell. As with each time before, Patrick, the butler answered. He looked a bit surprised to see four officers standing there. "Can I help you?"

"I'm sure you remember me," Nathan said.

"I do. What do you want this time?"

"We are here for Father Mike. Is he here?"

"The family is just sitting down to brunch. Can't this wait?"

Nathan nodded to the other officers, who then pushed their way past Patrick, with Nathan on his crutches slowly bringing up the rear.

"What's the meaning of this?" Mr. Parker said, when the officers entered the dining room. Father Mike was sitting on the far side of the table. Denzinger and Hank walked over and stood behind him.

"Michael Dunbar, you're under arrest for the murders of Ann Parker and Elizabeth Howe and the assault on Isabella Osborne," Nathan said.

"What?" Father Mike said.

Mrs. Parker let out a gasp, nearly falling out of her chair. "William, what is he talking about?"

William Parker stood. "What is the meaning of this? Father Mike didn't do that. He wouldn't do such a thing."

"Mr. Parker, please sit down," Nathan said. "Gloria, read Father Mike his rights."

While Gloria read him his rights, Denzinger and Hank handcuffed Father Mike. "Do you understand your rights as I have read them to you?" Gloria finished.

"I do," Father Mike replied.

"Having these rights in mind, do you wish to talk to us now?" she asked

"This has weighed heavy on my mind and in my heart," Father Mike said. "I'm guilty of what you said. Margaret, I'm so sorry."

Upon hearing that, Mrs. Parker fainted, falling out of her chair to the floor. Mr. Parker immediately was at her side. "Patrick, call an ambulance!"

"William, I'm sorry. I had no choice," the priest continued.

"Take him to another room," Nathan said. Denzinger and Hank led the priest out of the dining room, and to Mr. Parker's den. "Gloria, would you wait with the Parkers for the ambulance?"

Gloria shook her head. Nathan limped out of the room to join the officers. In the den, Father Mike was leaning against the desk.

"Wouldn't you be more comfortable sitting?" Nathan asked, coming into the room.

"I prefer to stand."

"Do you want to tell us what happened?"

Father Mike closed his eyes for a few seconds before beginning. "Ann had turned away from the church, and toward paganism. She was becoming a Wicca. I tried to steer her back to our church, the church she grew up in, and the church that she once loved.

"I went to see Ann in Mystic one day. She wasn't home, but a neighbor told me where she worked in town. I went there."

"To the Magick Potions, and Gifts store?"

"Yes. It literally hurt my soul when I walked in. She saw me, and immediately took me out onto the sidewalk to talk. She told me I didn't understand; that I was wrong, and told me to leave. I came back at the store's closing time. When she came out, I grabbed her by the arm. She didn't fight me at first. I showed her that I had a knife, and told her to come with me."

"Where did you take her?" Nathan asked.

"I made her drive us to the cemetery. I only wanted to scare her." He began to cry.

"What happened then?"

"It was an accident. I swear. I only wanted to scare her. I reminded her about what they did to witches in Salem. I put the rope around her neck." Tears ran down his cheek. "I rigged the rope so it wouldn't really strangle her, but she couldn't struggle, and I told her not to. I pulled on the rope to raise her off the ground. She didn't listen, and began to struggle to get free. The rope slipped around her neck. By the time I got her to the ground, she was gone." Father Mike's legs gave out and he fell to his knees. "God, please forgive me." He was sobbing.

Denzinger and Hank helped Father Mike to the couch.

"Why didn't you call an ambulance?" Nathan asked.

"I had just killed my niece. I couldn't go to jail for that."

"Tell me about the cat blood."

"In the Bible, the sprinkling of blood around a temple represents life cleansing the death of sin. I was cleansing her of sin."

Nathan looked at Denzinger and Hank. He could only shake his head. "What about Elizabeth Howe? Why did you kill her?"

"She saw me leave with Ann. Once Ann's body would be found, I would be on the spot. I had to get rid of her too. She was a witch, too. She had to be dealt with."

Nathan had heard enough. "Hank, ask Sergeant Donnelly and Officer Avery take him back to Mystic and book him for the murders and Isabella's assault."

Hank took him out of the room. Nathan and Denzinger went back into the dining room. The paramedics were just taking Mrs. Parker out. Mr. Parker was still in shock as he walked out of the room with the paramedics. Nathan briefly stopped him. "We have a warrant to search Father Mike's residence."

"What? Oh, of course. Patrick, take them out back to Father Mike's house." He then walked out to the ambulance to be with his wife.

The rest of the officers and Mallory searched the pool house where Father Mike lived. In there, they found Ann, Elizabeth, and Isabella's missing amulets inside of a Bible.

The next morning, Nathan made sure he was at roll call for two special announcements. The other officers made sure there was a vacant seat for him to sit. Hank sat on one side of him, an empty chair was on the other side.

"I kept forgetting to ask, did you hear anything about how Joe Cassidy is after his problem here at the department?" Hank quietly asked.

"As a matter of fact, I called him this morning. He said once he got to the hospital and received his insulin, he was fine."

Witch Hunt

Sergeant Donnelly finished with his briefing, allowing Chief Cabot stepped to the podium. Mayor Cranston came into the room and stood behind Chief Cabot.

He cleared his throat before he began. "I have a few announcements to make before you all hit the road this morning. First, we're all glad to see Detective Perry here today. He'll be going on medical leave later today to have his knee fixed." The officers broke into applause. "Mallory Duncan, would you step forward."

The officers moved aside so Mallory could join the chief.

"I can't begin to tell you what your work in forensics for this department has done to help with the prompt solving of crimes in this city. I'm honored and pleased to inform you, and everyone else, that we were notified that the grant for a new forensics lab, and an assistant, was approved. You should be very proud." He handed her the letter of notification.

Mallory smiled from ear to ear, as the room applauded. She looked at Nathan and gave him a wink. She stepped down and went back to her seat.

"All right, quiet down," the chief said. "I have one more announcement. Officer Gloria Wheeler, would you step forward."

Gloria eyes widened upon hearing her name, and she looked confused as she stepped to the front of the room. Nathan saw that her husband had sneaked in and was now sitting next to him. She reached the front of the room and stood next to the chief.

"It has been no secret that in the past, I've not been so accommodating to female officers. We have ten female officers within the department, with only one being a patrol officer. It's time to add another. Officer Wheeler, you have proved to be a valuable asset to this department with your assistance to Detective Perry in his cases."

Gloria looked over to Nathan, then saw her husband sitting next to him.

"It's my honor to announce that you are immediately

being promoted to the rank of corporal and transferred to the patrol division."

The whole room erupted into applause and cheers. Gloria couldn't contain herself, tears rolling down her cheek.

"Quiet, quiet," the chief said. "You'll be assigned to a training officer during your probation period, and will still assist Detective Perry in his investigations, after he returns from medical leave. That concludes our roll call today. Hit the roads, men---er, officers." The chief turned to talk to the mayor, who was offering her congratulations to Gloria.

Nathan shook hands with Gloria's husband, Steve. "You should be very proud of your wife."

"I am. She's been waiting a long time for this." Gloria ran over and hugged her husband.

"Congratulations, Gloria. You deserved this so much," Nathan said.

"Thank you." She showed them the new stripes she was given.

Epilogue

The next morning, Dana drove Nathan to the airport for his trip to Washington, D.C. to meet with the doctors at Walter Reed Hospital about his leg. It was a quiet ride, with neither knowing for sure what to say.

"I wish you'd let me go with you," Dana finally said. "How will you navigate the airport when you arrive in D.C."

Nathan hadn't wanted go into details with Dana, so he kept it short. "Katherine is going to pick me up."

"Your former girlfriend will be picking you up? Will she be taking you straight to the hospital?"

"I'm not due there until Monday," he said.

Dana didn't respond. A few miles down the road, she asked, "Where will you be staying?"

Nathan let out a deep breath. "Until we find out what my treatment plan is, I will be staying with her and Simon."

"I see. At least you can spend some time with your son."

He knew he was in trouble. Dana pulled up to the airport terminal. She got out to get his backpack for him, and helped him get it onto his back. She stretched up to give him a kiss. "Be careful and good luck. Please call me as soon as you know what the plan is for your knee."

"I will. Thanks for helping me this week." He gave her a tight hug and then went inside the terminal.

****

Later that day, Isabella sat at the desk in the office of her shop. Darius came in to pick her up from work. "Are you ready to go home?"

"I just need to do one more thing. Nathan did such a wonderful thing finding out who killed Ann and Elizabeth, and attacked me, that I want to do something nice for him." She placed a set of hugging ghosts on her desk. They were like the one that Nathan had purchased for Dana.

"What are you going to do?" Darius asked.

"I'm going to cast a love spell for him, to find someone that will make him happy."

"You sure you want to do that? It's normally not good to cast a spell on someone without their permission."

"It'll be fine."

As she began her chant, she twisted a red ribbon around the ghosts binding them together.

"Love is his heart's desire,
I pull in the Element of Fire,
The love he needs, put in his heart,
Make it grow, give it spark,
Don't make him wait. Send it fast,
Bring to him love that will last."

About the Author

Carol Preflatish lives in southern Indiana, and is the author of the Nathan Perry Mystery series. Carol started her career in 2010 writing romantic suspense novels. After switching genres to mystery, she released the Nathan Perry Mystery Series. When she's not writing, she loves to read, watch Indianapolis Colts football, and do just about anything outdoors.

An avid photographer, Carol has had many of her photos published. She is most proud to have had photos appear in Golf Journal, the official publication of the United States Golf Association. A few little-known facts about Carol are that she's a licensed amateur radio operator, has a degree in Physical Education, and is a collector of celebrity autographs, stamps, and coins.

Carol is a member of Sisters in Crime Writing Association, SinC's Guppies chapter, and a member of the Louisville, Kentucky SinC chapter. She also belongs to the Kentuckiana Authors group.

You can learn more about Carol by visiting her web page at http://CarolPre.com

www.ingramcontent.com/pod-product-compliance
Lightning Source LLC
Chambersburg PA
CBHW031224260626

47169CB00007B/2179